Wendy Hanniford. A sex-hungry seductress with an all-devouring appetite for older men? Or a lost little girl looking for the father she never had?

Richie Vanderpoel. A pretty boy who cruised the gay underground, taking a different lover every night? Or a young man terrified of his own real desires?

Both of them were dead. Maybe everyone knew who did it and how it happened. But did anyone know why . . .

LAWRENCE BLOCK
THE SINS OF THE FATHERS

A JOVE BOOK

THE SINS OF THE FATHERS

A Jove Book / published by arrangement with
the author

PRINTING HISTORY
Dell edition / August 1976
Jove edition / October 1982
Fifth printing / October 1984

ISBN: 0-515-08157-4

Jove books are published by The Berkley Publishing Group,
200 Madison Avenue, New York, N.Y. 10016.
The words "A JOVE BOOK" and the "J" with sunburst
are trademarks belonging to Jove Publications, Inc.

PRINTED IN THE UNITED STATES OF AMERICA

ONE

He was a big man, about my height with a little more flesh on his heavy frame. His eyebrows, arched and prominent, were still black. The hair on his head was iron gray, combed straight back, giving his massive head a leonine appearance. He had been wearing glasses but had placed them on the oak table between us. His dark brown eyes kept searching my face for secret messages. If he found any, his eyes didn't reflect them. His features were sharply chiseled—a hawk-bill nose, a full mouth, a craggy jawline—but the full effect of his face was as a blank stone tablet waiting for someone to scratch commandments on it.

He said, "I don't know very much about you, Scudder."

I knew a little about him. His name was Cale Hanniford. He was around fifty-five years old. He lived upstate in Utica where he had a wholesale drug business and some real estate holdings. He had last year's Cadillac parked outside at the curb. He had a wife waiting for him in his room at the Carlyle.

1

He had a daughter in a cold steel drawer at the city mortuary.

"There's not much to know," I said. "I used to be a cop."

"An excellent one, according to Lieutenant Koehler."

I shrugged.

"And now you're a private detective."

"No."

"I thought—"

"Private detectives are licensed. They tap telephones and follow people. They fill out forms, they keep records, all of that. I don't do those things. Sometimes I do favors for people. They give me gifts."

"I see."

I took a sip of coffee. I was drinking coffee spiked with bourbon. Hanniford had a Dewar's and water in front of him but wasn't taking much interest in it. We were in Armstrong's, a good sound saloon with dark wood walls and a stamped tin ceiling. It was two in the afternoon on the second Tuesday in January, and we had the place pretty much to ourselves. A couple of nurses from Roosevelt Hospital were nursing beers at the far end of the bar, and a kid with a tentative beard was eating a hamburger at one of the window tables.

He said, "It's difficult for me to explain what I want you to do for me, Scudder."

"I'm not sure that there's anything I *can* do for you. Your daughter is dead. I can't change that. The boy who killed her was picked up on the spot. From what I read in the papers, it couldn't be more open-and-shut if they had the homicide on film." His face darkened; he was seeing that film

2

now, the knife slashing. I went on quickly. "They picked him up and booked him and slapped him in the Tombs. That was Thursday?" He nodded. "And Saturday morning they found him hanging in his cell. Case closed."

"Is that your view? That the case is closed?"

"From a law enforcement standpoint."

"That's not what I meant. Of course the police have to see it that way. They apprehended the killer, and he's beyond punishment." He leaned forward. "But there are things I have to know."

"Like what?"

"I want to know why she was killed. I want to know who she was. I've had no real contact with Wendy in the past three years. Christ, I didn't even know for certain that she was living in New York." His eyes slipped away from mine. "They say she didn't have a job. No apparent source of income. I saw the building she lived in. I wanted to go up to her apartment, but I couldn't. Her rent was almost four hundred dollars a month. What does that suggest to you?"

"That some man was paying her rent."

"She shared that apartment with the Vanderpoel boy. The boy who killed her. He worked for an antiques importer. He earned something in the neighborhood of a hundred and twenty-five dollars a week. If a man were keeping her as his mistress, he wouldn't let her have Vanderpoel as a roommate, would he?" He drew a breath. "I guess it must be fairly obvious that she was a prostitute. The police didn't tell me that in so many words. They were tactful. The newspapers were somewhat less tactful."

They usually are. And the case was the kind the newspapers like to play with. The girl was attractive, the murder took place in the Village, and there was a nice core of sex to it. And they had picked up Richard Vanderpoel running in the streets with her blood all over him. No city editor worth a damn would let that one slide past him.

He said, "Scudder? Do you see why the case isn't closed for me?"

"I guess I do." I made myself look deep into his dark eyes. "The murder was a door starting to open for you. Now you have to know what's inside the room."

"Then you do understand."

I did, and wished I didn't. I had not wanted the job. I work as infrequently as I can. I had no present need to work. I don't need much money. My room rent is cheap, my day-to-day expenses low enough. Besides, I had no reason to dislike this man. I have always felt more comfortable taking money from men I dislike.

"Lieutenant Koehler didn't understand what I wanted. I'm sure he only gave me your name as a polite way of getting rid of me." That wasn't all there was to it, but I let it pass. "But I really need to know these things. Who was she? Who did Wendy turn into? And why would anyone want to kill her?"

Why did anyone want to kill anybody? The act of murder is performed four or five times a day in New York. One hot week last summer the count ran to fifty-three. People kill their friends, their relatives, their lovers. A man on Long Island demonstrated karate to his older children by chopping his two-year-old daughter to death. Why did people do these things?

Cain said he wasn't Abel's keeper. Are those the only choices, keeper or killer?

4

"Will you work for me, Scudder?" He managed a small smile. "I'll rephrase that. Will you do me a favor? And it would be a favor."

"I wonder if that's true."

"How do you mean?"

"That open door. There might be things in that room you won't want to look at."

"I know that."

"And that's why you have to."

"That's right."

I finished my coffee. I put the cup down and took a deep breath. "Yeah," I said, "I'll give it a shot."

He settled into his chair, took out a pack of cigarettes and lit one. It was his first since he'd walked in. Some people reach for a cigarette when they're tense, others when the tension passes. He was looser now, and looked as though he felt he had accomplished something.

I had a new cup of coffee in front of me and a couple of pages filled in my notebook. Hanniford was still working on the same drink. He had told me a lot of things I would never need to know about his daughter. But any of the things he said might turn out to matter, and there was no way to guess which it might be. I had learned long ago to listen to everything a man had to say.

So I learned that Wendy was an only child, that she had done well in high school, that she had been popular with her classmates but had not dated much. I was getting a picture of a girl, not sharply defined, but a picture that would eventually have to find a way of blending with one of a slashed-up whore in a Village apartment.

The picture started to blur when she went away

to college in Indiana. That was evidently when they began to lose her. She majored in English, minored in government. A couple of months before she was due to graduate she packed a suitcase and disappeared.

"The school got in touch with us. I was very worried, she had never done anything like this before. I didn't know what to do. Then we had a postcard. She was in New York, she had a job, there were some things she had to work out. We had another card several months after that from Miami. I didn't know whether she had moved there or was vacationing."

And then nothing until the telephone rang and they learned she was dead. She was seventeen when she finished high school, twenty-one when she dropped out of college, twenty-four when Richard Vanderpoel cut her up. That was as old as she was ever going to get.

He began telling me things I would learn over again in more detail from Koehler. Names, addresses, dates, times. I let him talk. Something bothered me, and I let it sort itself out in my mind.

He said, "The boy who killed her. Richard Vanderpoel. He was younger than she was. He was only twenty." He frowned at a memory. "When I heard what happened, what he had done, I wanted to kill that boy. I wanted to put him to death with my hands." His hands tightened into fists at the recollection, then opened slowly. "But after he committed suicide, I don't know, something changed inside me. It struck me that he was a victim, too. His father is a minister."

"Yes, I know."

"A church in Brooklyn somewhere. I had an impulse. I wanted to talk to the man. I don't know what I thought I might want to say to him. Whatever it was, after a moment's reflection I realized I could never have that conversation. And yet—''

"You want to know the boy. In order to know your daughter."

He nodded.

I said, "Do you know what an Identikit portrait is, Mr. Hanniford? You've probably seen them in newspaper stories. When the police have an eyewitness, they use this kit of transparent overlays to piece together a composite picture of a suspect. 'Is this nose like this? Or is this one more like it? Bigger? Wider? How about the ears? Which set of ears comes the closest?' And so on until the features add up to a face.''

"Yes, I've seen how that works."

"Then you've probably also seen actual photographs of the suspect side by side with the Identikit portraits. They never seem to resemble one another, especially to the untrained eye. But there is a *factual* resemblance, and a trained officer can often make very good use of it. Do you see what I'm getting at? You want photographs of your daughter and the boy who killed her. I'm not equipped to offer you that. No one is. I can dig up enough facts and impressions to make composite Identikit portraits for you, but the result may not be all that close to what you really want."

"I understand."

"You want me to go ahead?"

"Yes. Definitely."

"I'm probably more expensive than one of the big agencies. They'd work for you either per diem or on an hourly basis. Plus expenses. I take a certain amount of money and pay my own expenses out of it. I don't like keeping records. I also don't like writing reports, or checking in periodically when there's nothing to say for the sake of keeping a client contented."

"How much money do you want?"

I never know how to set prices. How do you put a value on your time when its only value is personal? And when your life has been deliberately restructured to minimize involvement in the lives of others, how much do you charge the man who forces you to involve yourself?

"I want two thousand dollars from you now. I don't know how long this will take or when you'll decide you've seen enough of the dark room. I may ask you for more money somewhere along the way, or after it's over. Of course you always have the option of not paying me."

He smiled suddenly. "You're a very unorthodox businessman."

"I suppose so."

"I've never had occasion to hire a detective, so I don't really know how this is usually done. Do you mind a check?"

I told him a check was fine, and while he was writing it out, I figured out what had been bothering me earlier. I said, "You never hired detectives after Wendy disappeared from college?"

"No." He looked up. "It wasn't that long before we received the first of the two postcards. I'd considered hiring detectives, of course, but once we knew she was all right I dropped the idea."

"But you still didn't know where she was, or how she was living."

"No." He lowered his eyes. "That's part of it, of course. Why I'm busy now, locking up the empty stable." His eyes returned to mine, and there was something in them that I wanted to turn from, and couldn't. "I have to know how much to blame myself."

Did he really think he would ever have the answer to that one? Oh, he might find himself an answer, but it would not be the right answer. There is never a right answer to that inescapable question.

He finished writing the check and passed it to me. He had left space blank where my name belonged. He told me he thought I might like it made out to *Cash*. I said payable to me was fine, and he uncapped his pen again and wrote *Matthew Scudder* on the right line. I folded it and put it in my wallet.

I said, "Mr. Hanniford, there's something you left out. You don't think it's important, but it might be, and you think it might be."

"How do you know that?"

"Instinct, I suppose. I spent a lot of years watching people decide how close they cared to come to the truth. There's nothing you *have* to tell me, but—"

"Oh, it's extraneous, Scudder. I left it out because I didn't think it fit in, but—Oh, the hell with it. Wendy's not my biological daughter."

"She was adopted?"

"I adopted her. My wife is Wendy's mother. Wendy's father was killed before Wendy was born, he was a Marine, he died in the landing at Inchon." He looked away again. "I married Wendy's mother three years after that. From the beginning I loved her as much as any real father could have. When I found out that I was . . . unable to father children myself, I was even more grateful for her existence. Well? Is it important?"

9

"I don't know," I said. "Probably not." But of course it was important to me. It told me something more about Hanniford's load of guilt.

"Scudder? You're not married, are you?"

"Divorced."

"Any children?"

I nodded. He started to say something, and didn't. I began wanting him to leave.

He said, "You must have been a very good policeman."

"I wasn't bad. I had cop instincts, and I learned the moves. That's at least ninety percent of it."

"How long were you on the force?"

"Fifteen years. Almost sixteen."

"Isn't there a pension or something if you stay twenty?"

"That's right."

He didn't ask the question, and that was strangely more annoying than if he had.

I said, "I lost the faith."

"Like a priest?"

"Something like that. Not exactly, because it's not rare for a cop to lose the faith and go on being a cop. He may never have had it in the first place. What it amounted to was that I found out I didn't want to be a cop anymore." Or a husband, or a father. Or a productive member of society.

"All the corruption in the department? That sort of thing?"

"No, no." The corruption had never bothered me. I would have found it hard to support a family without it. "No, it was something else."

"I see."

"You do? Hell, it's not a secret. I was off duty one night in the summer. I was in a bar in Washington heights where cops didn't have to pay

10

for their drinks. Two kids held up the place. On their way out they shot the bartender in the heart. I chased them into the street. I shot one of them dead and caught the other in the thigh. He's never going to walk right again."

"I see."

"No, I don't think you do. That wasn't the first time I ever killed anyone. I was glad the one died and sorry the other recovered."

"Then—"

"One shot went wide and ricocheted. It hit a seven-year-old girl in the eye. The ricochet took most of the steam off the bullet. An inch higher and it probably would have glanced off her forehead. Would have left a nasty scar but nothing much worse than that. This way, though, nothing but soft tissue, and it went right on into her brain. They tell me she died instantly." I looked at my hands. The tremor was barely visible. I picked up my cup and drained it. I said, "There was no question of culpability. As a matter of fact, I got a departmental commendation. Then I resigned. I just didn't want to be a cop anymore."

I sat there for a few minutes after he left. Then I caught Trina's eye and she brought over another cup of laced coffee. "Your friend's not much of a drinker," she said.

I agreed that he wasn't. Something in my tone must have alerted her because she sat down in Hanniford's chair and put her hand on top of mine for a moment.

"Troubles, Matt?"

"Not really. Things to do, and I'd rather not do them."

"You'd rather just sit here and get drunk."

I grinned at her. "When did you ever see me drunk?"

"Never. And I never saw you when you weren't drinking."

"It's a nice middle ground."

"Can't be good for you, can it?"

I wished she would touch my hand again. Her fingers were long and slender, her touch very cool. "Nothing's much good for anybody," I said.

"Coffee and booze. It's a very weird combination."

"Is it?"

"Booze to get you drunk, and coffee to keep you sober."

I shook my head. "Coffee never sobered anybody. It just keeps you awake. Give a drunk plenty of coffee and you've got a wide-awake drunk on your hands."

"That what you are, baby? A wide-awake drunk?"

"I'm neither," I told her. "That's what keeps me drinking."

I got to my savings bank a little after four. I stuck five hundred in my account and took the rest of Hanniford's money in cash. It was my first visit since the first of the year, so they entered some interest in my passbook. A machine figured it all out in the wink of an eye. The sum involved was hardly large enough to warrant wasting the machine's time on it.

I walked back on Fifty-seventh Street to Ninth, then headed uptown past Armstrong's and the hospital to St. Paul's. Mass was just winding up, and I waited outside while a couple dozen people straggled out of the church. They were mostly middle-aged women. Then I went inside and slipped four fifty-dollar bills into the poor box.

I tithe. I don't know why. It's become a habit, as indeed it has become my habit to visit churches. I began doing this shortly after I moved into my hotel room.

I like churches. I like to sit in them when I have things to think about. I sat around the middle of this one on the aisle. I suppose I was there for twenty minutes, maybe a little longer.

Two thousand dollars from Cale Hanniford to me, two hundred dollars from me to St. Paul's poor box. I don't know what they do with the money. Maybe it buys food and clothing for poor families. Maybe it buys Lincolns for the clergy. I don't really care what they do with it.

The Catholics get more of my money than anybody else. Not because I'm partial to them, but because they put in longer hours. Most of the Protestants close up shop during the week.

One big plus for the Catholics, though. You get to light candles. I lit three on the way out. For Wendy Hanniford, who would never get to be twenty-five, and for Richard Vanderpoel, who would never get to be twenty-one. And, of course, for Estrellita Rivera, who would never get to be eight.

TWO

The Sixth Precinct is on West Tenth Street. Eddie Koehler was in his office reading reports when I got there. He didn't look surprised to see me. He pushed some papers to one side, nodded at the chair alongside his desk. I settled into it and reached over to shake hands with him. Two tens and a five passed smoothly from my hand to his.

"You look like you need a new hat," I told him.

"I do indeed. One thing I can always use is another hat. How'd you like Hanniford?"

"Poor bastard."

"Yeah, that's about it. It all happened so quick he's left standing there with his jaw hanging. That's what did it for him, you know. The time element. If it takes us a week or a month to make a collar, say. Or if there's a trial, and it drags on for a year or so. That way things keep going on for him, it gives him a chance to get used to what happened while it's all still in process. But this way, bam, one thing after another, we got the killer in a cell before he even hears his daughter's dead, and by the time he gets his ass in gear the kid hangs himself, and Hanniford can't get used to it because he's had no time." He eyed me speculatively. "So I figured an old buddy could make a couple of bills out of it."

"Why not?"

He took a cold cigar out of the ashtray and relit it. He could have afforded a fresh one. The Sixth is a hot precinct, and his desk was a good one. He could also have afforded to send Hanniford home instead of referring him to me so that I could knock back twenty-five to him. Old habits die hard.

"Get yourself a clipboard, bounce around the neighborhood, ask some questions. Run yourself a week's work out of it without wasting more'n a couple of hours. Hit him up for a hundred a day plus expenses. That's close to a K for you, for Christ's sake."

I said, "I'd like a look at your file on the thing."

"Why go through the motions? You're not gonna find anything there, Matt. It was closed before it was opened. We had cuffs on the fucking kid before we even knew what he did."

"Just for form."

His eyes narrowed just a little. We were about the same age, but I had joined the force earlier and was just getting into plainclothes when he was going through the Academy. Koehler looked a lot older now, droopy in the jowls, and his desk job was spreading him in the seat. There was something about his eyes I didn't care for.

"Waste of time, Matt. Why take the trouble?"

"Let's say it's the way I work."

"Files aren't open to unauthorized personnel. You know that."

I said, "Let's say another hat for a look at what you've got. And I'll want to talk to the arresting officer."

"I could set that up, arrange an introduction. Whether he wants to talk to you is up to him."

"Sure."

Twenty minutes later I was alone in the office. I had twenty-five dollars less in my wallet and a manila folder on the desk in front of me. It didn't look like good value for the money, didn't tell me much I didn't already know.

Patrolman Lewis Pankow, the arresting officer, led off with his report. I hadn't read one of those in a while, and it took me back, from "While proceeding in a westerly direction on routine foot patrol duty" all the way through to "at which time the alleged perpetrator was delivered for incarceration to the Men's House of Detention." The Coptic jargon is a special one.

I read Pankow's report a couple of times through and took some notes. What it amounted to, in English, was a clear enough statement of facts. At eighteen minutes after four he'd been walking west on Bank Street. He heard sounds of a commotion and shortly encountered some people who told him there was a lunatic on Bethune Street, dancing around with blood all over him. Pankow ran around the block to Bethune Street where he found "the alleged miscreant, subsequently identified as Richard Vanderpoel of 194 Bethune Street, his clothes in disarray and covered with what appeared to be blood, uttering obscene language at high volume and exposing his private parts to passersby.''

Pankow sensibly cuffed him and managed to determine where he lived. He led the suspect up two flights of stairs and into the apartment Vanderpoel and Wendy Hanniford had occupied, where he found Wendy Hanniford "apparently deceased, unclothed, and disfigured by slashes apparently inflicted by a sharp weapon.''

Pankow then phoned in, and the usual machinery went into action. The medical examiner's man had come around to confirm what Pankow had figured out—that Wendy was, in fact, dead. The photo crew took their pictures, several of the blood-spattered apartment, a great many of Wendy's corpse.

There was no telling what she might have looked like alive. She had died from loss of blood, and Lady Macbeth was right about that; no one would guess how much blood a body can lose in the process of dying. You can put an ice pick in a man's heart and barely a drop of blood will show on his shirtfront, but Vanderpoel had cut her breasts and thighs and belly and throat, and the whole bed was an ocean of blood.

After they'd photographed the body, they removed it for autopsy. A Dr. Jainchill of the medical examiner's office had done the full postmortem. He stated that the victim was a Caucasian female in her twenties, that she had had recent sexual intercourse, both oral and genital, that she had been slashed twenty-three times with a sharp instrument, most probably a razor, that there were no stab wounds (which might have been why he was opting for the razor), that various veins and arteries, which he conscientiously named, had been wholly or partially severed in the course of this mistreatment, that death had occurred at approximately four o'clock that afternoon, give or take twenty minutes, and that there was in his opinion no possibility whatsoever that the wounds had been self-inflicted.

I was proud of him for taking such a firm stand on the last point.

The rest of the folder consisted of bits of information which would ultimately be supplemented by copies of formal reports filed by other branches of the machine. There was a note to the effect that the prisoner had been brought before a magistrate and formally charged with homicide the day after his arrest. Another memo gave the name of the court-appointed attorney. Another noted that Richard Vanderpoel had been found dead in his cell shortly before six Saturday morning.

The folder would grow fatter in time to come. The case was closed, but the Sixth's file would go on growing like a corpse's hair and fingernails. The guard who looked in and saw Richard Vanderpoel hanging from the steam pipe would write up his findings. So would the physician who pronounced him dead and the physician who established beyond a shadow of a doubt that it was the strips of bedclothing tied together and knotted around his neck that had done him in. Ultimately a coroner's inquest would conclude that Wendy Hanniford had been murdered by Richard Vanderpoel and that Richard Vanderpoel had in turn taken his own life. The Sixth Precinct, and everyone else connected with the case, had already reached this conclusion. They had reached the first part of it well before Vanderpoel had been booked. The case was closed.

I went back and read through some of the material again. I studied the photos in turn. The apartment itself didn't look to be greatly disturbed, which suggested the killer had been someone known to her. I went back to the autopsy. No skin under Wendy's fingernails, no obvious signs of a struggle. Facial contusions? Yes, so she could have been unconscious while he cut her up.

She had probably been awhile dying. If he'd cut the throat first, and got the jugular right, she would have gone fast. But she had lost a lot of blood from the wounds on the torso.

I picked out one print and tucked it inside my shirt. I wasn't sure why I wanted it but knew it would never be missed. I knew a desk cop in the Cobble Hill section of Brooklyn who used to take home a copy of every grisly picture he could get his hands on. I never asked why.

I had everything back in order and returned to the file folder by the time Koehler came back. He had a fresh cigar going. I got out from behind his desk. He asked me if I was satisfied.

"I'd still like to talk to Pankow."

"I already set it up. I figured you're too fucking stubborn to change your mind. You find a single damn thing in that mess?"

"How do I know? I don't even know what I'm looking for. I understand she was hooking. Any evidence of that?"

"Nothing hard. There would be if we looked. Good wardrobe, couple hundred in her handbag, no visible means of support. What's that add up to?"

"Why was she living with Vanderpoel?"

"He had a twelve-inch tongue."

"Seriously. Was he pimping for her?"

"Probably."

"You didn't have a sheet on either of them, though."

"No. No arrest. They didn't exist officially for us until he decided to cut her up."

I closed my eyes for a minute. Koehler said my name. I looked up. I said, "Just a thought. Something you said before about time putting Hanniford on the spot. It's true in a way besides the one you mentioned. If she was killed by person or persons unknown, you'd have put the past two years of her life on slides and run them through a microscope. But it was over before it started, and it's not your job to do that now."

"Right. So it's your job instead."

"Uh-huh. What did he kill her with?"

"Doc says a razor." He shrugged. "Good a guess as any."

"What happened to the murder weapon?"

"Yeah, I figured you wouldn't miss that. We didn't turn it up. You can't make much out of that. There was a window open, he could have pitched it out."

"What's outside of the window?"

"Airshaft."

"You checked it?"

"Uh-huh. Anybody coulda picked it up, any kid passing through."

"Check for blood spots in the airshaft?"

"Are you kidding? An airshaft in the Village?

People piss out windows, they throw Tampax out, garbage, everything. Nine out of ten airshafts you'll find blood spots. Would you have checked? With the killer already wrapped up?"

"No."

"Anyway, forget the airshaft. He bolts out of the apartment with the knife in his hand. Or the razor, whatever the fuck it was. He drops it on the staircase. He runs out in the street and drops it on the sidewalk. He puts it in an open garbage can. He drops it down a sewer. Matt, we don't have an eyewitness who saw him come out of the building. We woulda turned one up if we needed one, but the son of a bitch was dead thirty-six hours after he cooled the girl."

It kept coming back to that. I was doing a job the police would have done if they had had to do it. But Richard Vanderpoel had saved them the trouble.

"So we don't know when he hit the street," Koehler was saying. "Two minutes before Pankow got to him? Ten minutes? He coulda chewed up the knife and ate it in that amount of time. Christ knows he was crazy enough."

"Was there a razor in the apartment?"

"You mean a straight razor? No."

"I mean a man's razor."

"Yeah, he had an electric. Why the hell don't you forget about the razor? You know what those fucking autopsies are like. I had one a couple years ago, the asshole in the medical examiner's office said the victim had been killed with a hatchet. We already caught the bastard on the premises with a croquet mallet in his hand. Anybody who could mistake the damage done by splitting someone's skull with a hatchet and beating it in with a mallet couldn't tell a razor slash from a cunt.''

I nodded. I said, ''I wonder why he did it.''

''Because he was out of his fucking mind, that's why he did it. He ran up and down the street covered with her blood, screaming his head off and waving his cock at the world. Ask him why he did it and he wouldn't know himself.''

''What a world.''

''Jesus, don't let me get started on that. This neighborhood gets worse and worse. Don't get me started.'' He gave me a nod, and we walked together out of his office and out through the squad room. Men in plainclothes and men in uniforms sat at typewriters, laboriously pounding out stories about presumed miscreants and alleged perpetrators. A woman was making a report in Spanish to a uniformed officer, pausing intermittently to weep. I wonder what she had done or what had been done to her.

I didn't see anybody in the squad room that I recognized.

Koehler said, ''You hear about Barney Segal? They made it permanent. He's head of the Seventeenth.''

''Well, he's a good man.''

''One of the best. How long you been off the force, Matt?''

''Couple of years, I guess.''

''Yeah. How're Anita and the boys? Doing okay?''

''They're fine.''

''You keep in touch, then.''

''From time to time.''

As we neared the front desk he stopped, cleared his throat. "You ever think about putting the badge back on, Matt?"

"No way, Eddie."

"That's a goddam shame, you know that?"

"You do what you have to do."

"Yeah." He drew himself up and got back to business. "I set it with Pankow so he'll be looking for you around nine tonight. He'll be at a bar called Johnny Joyce's. It's on Second Avenue, I forget the cross street."

"I know the place."

"They know him there, so just ask the bartender to point him out to you. He's on his own time tonight, so I told him you'd make it worth his while."

And told him to make sure a piece of it came back to the lieutenant, no doubt.

"Matt?" I turned. "What the hell are you gonna ask him, anyway?"

"I want to know what obscene language Vanderpoel was using."

"Seriously?" I nodded. "I think you're as crazy as Vanderpoel," he told me. "For the price of a hat you can hear all the dirty words in the world."

THREE

Bethune Street runs west from Hudson toward the river. It is narrow and residential. Some trees had been recently planted. Their bases were guarded by little picket fences hung with signs imploring dog owners to thwart their pets' natural instincts. WE LOVE OUR TREE/PLEASE CURB YOUR DOG. Number 194 was a renovated brownstone with a front door the color of Astroturf. There were five apartments, one to a floor. A sixth bell in the vestibule was marked SUPERINTENDENT. I rang it and waited.

The woman who opened the door was around thirty-five. She wore a man's white shirt with the top two buttons open and a pair of stained and faded jeans. She was built like a fireplug. Her hair was short and seemed to have been hacked at randomly with a pair of dull shears. The effect was not displeasing, though. She stood in the doorway and looked up at me and decided within five seconds that I was a cop. I gave her my name and learned that hers was Elizabeth Antonelli. I told her I wanted to talk to her.

"What about?"

"Your third-floor tenants."

"Shit. I thought that was over and done with. I'm still waiting for you guys to unlock the door and clear their stuff out. The landlord wants me to show the apartment, and I can't even get into it."

"It's still padlocked?"

"Don't you guys talk to each other?"

"I'm not on the force. This is private."

Her eyes did a number. She liked me better now that I wasn't a cop, but now she had to know what angle I was working. Also if I wasn't on official business, that meant she didn't have to feel compelled to waste her time on me.

She said, "Listen, I'm in the middle of something. I'm an artist, I got work to do."

"It'll take you less time to answer my questions than it will to get rid of me."

She thought this over, then turned abruptly and walked into the building. "It's freezing out there," she said. "C'mon downstairs, we'll talk, but don't figure on taking up too much of my time, huh?"

I followed her down a flight of stairs to the basement. She had a single large room with kitchen appliances in one corner and an army cot on the west wall. There were exposed pipes and electrical cables overhead. Her art was sculpture, and there were several examples of her work in evidence. I never saw the piece she was currently working on. A wet cloth was draped over it. The other pieces were abstract, and there was a massive quality to them, a ponderousness suggestive of sea monsters.

"I'm not going to be able to tell you much," she said. "I'm the super because I get a deal on the rent that way. I'm handy, I can fix most things that go wrong, and I'm mean enough to yell at people when they're late with the rent. Most of the time I keep to myself. I don't pay much attention to what goes on in the building."

"You knew Vanderpoel and Miss Hanniford?"

"By sight."

"When did they move in?"

"She was here before I moved in, and I've been here two years in April. He moved in with her I guess a little over a year ago. I think just before Christmas if I remember right."

"They didn't move in together?"

"No. She was living with someone else before that."

"A man?"

"A woman."

She didn't have any records, didn't know the name of Wendy's former roommate. She gave me the landlord's name and address. I asked her what she remembered about Wendy.

"Not a hell of a lot. I only notice people if they make trouble. She never had loud parties or played the stereo too loud. I was in the apartment a few times. The valve was shot on the bedroom radiator, and they were getting too much heat, they couldn't regulate it. I put a new valve in. That was just a couple of months ago."

"They kept the apartment neat?"

"Very neat. Very attractive. They had the trim painted, and the place was furnished nice." She thought for a moment. "I think maybe that was his doing. I was in the place before he moved in, and I think I remember it wasn't as nice then. He was sort of artsy."

"Did you know she was a prostitute?"

"I still don't know it. I read lots of lies in the papers."

"You don't think she was?"

"I don't have an opinion either way. I never had any complaints about her. Then again, she could have had ten men a day up there, and I wouldn't have known about it."

"Did she have visitors?"

"I just told you. I wouldn't know about it. People don't have to get past me to get upstairs."

I asked her who else lived in the building. There were five floor-through apartments, and she gave me the names of the tenants in each. I could talk to them if they were willing to talk to me, she said. But not the couple on the top floor—they were in Florida and wouldn't be back until the middle of March.

"You got enough?" she said. "I want to get back to what I was doing." She flexed her fingers, indicating an impatience to return them to the clay.

I told her she had been very helpful.

"I don't see that I told you anything much."

"There's something more you could tell me."

"What?"

"You didn't know them, either of them, and I realize you don't take much interest in the people in the building. But everybody invariably forms an impression of people they see frequently over an extended period of time. You must have had some sort of image of the two of them, some feeling that extended beyond your hard factual knowledge of them. That's probably been shifted out of position by what's happened in the past week, what you've learned about them, but I'd like to know what your impression of them was.''

"What good would that do you?''

"It would tell me what they looked like to human eyes. And you're an artist, you've got sensibilities.''

She gnawed at a fingernail. "Yeah, I see what you mean,'' she said after a moment. "I just can't find where to pick up on it.''

"You were surprised when he killed her.''

"Anybody'd be surprised.''

"Because it changed how you saw them. How did you see them?''

"Just as tenants, just ordinary—wait a minute. All right, you jarred something loose. I never even put words to the tune before, but you know how I thought of them? As brother and sister.''

"Brother and sister?''

"Right.''

"Why?''

She closed her eyes, frowned. "I can't say exactly,'' she said. "Maybe the way they acted when they were together. Not anything they did. Just the vibrations they gave off, the sense you got of them when they were walking along. The sense of how they related to each other.''

I waited.

"Another thing. I didn't dwell on this, I mean I didn't give it any thought to speak of, but I sort of took it for granted that he was gay.''

"Why?''

She had been sitting. She got up now and walked to one of her creations, a gunmetal-colored mound of convex planes taller and wider than herself. She faced away from me, tracing a curved surface with her stubby fingers.

"Physical type, I suppose. Mannerisms. He was tall and slender, he had a way of speaking. You'd think I would know better than to think in those terms. With my figure and short hair, and working with my hands, and being good with electrical and mechanical things. People generally assume I'm a lesbian." She turned around, and her eyes challenged me. "I'm not," she said.

"Was Wendy Hanniford?"

"How would I know?"

"You guessed Vanderpoel might be gay. Did you make the same guess about her?"

"Oh. I thought— No, I'm sure she wasn't. I generally know if a woman is gay by the way she relates to me. No, I assumed she was straight."

"And you assumed he wasn't."

"Right." She looked up at me. "You want to know something? I *still* think he was a faggot."

FOUR

I had some dinner in an Italian place on Green-wich Avenue, then hit a couple of bars before I took a cab over to Johnny Joyce's. I told the bar-tender I was looking for Lewis Pankow, and he pointed me toward a booth in the back.

I could have found him without help. He was tall and rangy and towheaded, with an open face and a recent shave. He stood up when I approached him. He was in civilian clothes, a gray glen-plaid suit that couldn't have cost him much, a pale blue shirt, a striped tie. I said I was Scudder, and he said he was Pankow, and he put out his hand, so I shook it. I sat down opposite him and ordered a double bourbon when the waiter came around. Pankow still had half a beer left in front of him.

He said, "The lieutenant said you wanted to see me. I guess it's about the Hanniford murder?"

I nodded. "Hell of a good collar for you."

"I was lucky. The right place at the right time."

"It'll look good on your record."

He flushed.

"Probably get a commendation out of it, too."

The flush deepened. I wondered how old he was. Say twenty-two at the outside. I thought about his report and decided he'd make detective third in a year or so.

I said, "I read your report. There was a lot of detail, but there were some things that you didn't have room for. When you got to the scene, Vanderpoel was standing about two doors from the building where the murder took place. Now what was he doing exactly? Dancing around? Running?"

"More or less standing in one place. But moving around wildly. Like he had a lot of energy he had to work off. Like when you drink too much coffee and your hands get shaky, but his whole body was like that."

"You said his clothing was disarrayed. How?"

"His shirttail was out of his pants. His belt was fastened, but his pants were unbuttoned and unzipped and his thing was hanging out."

"His penis?"

"Right, his penis."

"Was he exposing himself deliberately?"

"Well, it was hanging right out. He must of known about it."

"But he wasn't handling himself or thrusting out with his hips or anything like that?"

"No."

"Did he have an erection?"

"I didn't notice."

"You saw his cock and didn't notice if he had a hard-on or not?"

He flushed again. "He didn't have one."

31

The waiter brought my drink. I picked it up and looked into the glass. I said, "You put down that he was uttering obscenities."

"Shouting them. I heard him shouting before I even turned the corner."

"What was he saying?"

"You know."

He embarrassed easy, this one. I kept myself from snapping at him. "The words he used," I said.

"I don't like to use them."

"Force yourself."

He asked if it was important, and I said it might be. He leaned forward and pitched his voice low. "Motherfucker," he said.

"He just kept yelling motherfucker?"

"Not exactly."

"I want the words he used."

"Yeah, okay. What he said was, he kept yelling, 'I'm a motherfucker, I'm a motherfucker, I fucked my mother.' He kept shouting this over and over."

"He said he was a motherfucker and he fucked his mother."

"Right, that's what he said."

"What did you think?"

"I thought he was crazy."

"Did you think he killed someone?"

"Oh. No, the first thing I thought was he was hurt. He had blood all over him."

"His hands?"

"Everywhere. His hands, his shirt, his pants, his face, he was all covered with blood. I thought he was cut, but then I saw he was all right and the blood must of come from somebody else."

"How could you tell?"

"I just knew. He was all right, it wasn't his blood, so it was somebody else's." He hoisted his glass and drained it. I motioned for the waiter and ordered another beer for Pankow and a cup of coffee for myself. We sat there looking at the table until the waiter brought the order. Pankow was remembering things he'd spent the past few days trying to forget, and he wasn't enjoying it much.

I said, "So you expected to find a body in the apartment."

"I knew I would, yeah."

"Who did you think it would be?"

"Hell, I thought it would be his mother. From what he was saying, motherfucker, I fucked my mother, I thought he went nuts or something and killed his mother. I even thought that's who it was when I went in there, you know, on account of you couldn't tell age or anything at first, just this naked woman with blood everywhere, the sheets soaked, the blanket, all this very dark blood—"

His face was white tinged with green. I said, "Easy, Lew."

"I'm all right."

"I know you are. Put your head down between your knees. C'mon, swing out from behind the table and put your head down. You're all right."

"I know."

I thought he might faint, but he got hold of himself. He kept his head lowered for a minute or two, then sat up straight again. He had some color in his face now. He took a couple of deep breaths and a long swig of beer.

He said, "Jesus Christ."

"You're okay now."

"Yeah, right. I took one look at her lying there and I had to puke. I seen dead people before. My old man, he had a heart attack in his sleep, and I was the one walked in and found him. And since I joined the force, you know. But I never seen one like this and I hadda puke and I'm handcuffed to this asshole and he's still got his dick hanging out. I dragged the stupid bastard over to the corner and I just puked in the corner of the room, just like that, and what I did next, I had a fit of the giggles. I just couldn't help it, I stood there giggling like an idiot, and this guy cuffed to me, so help me God, he stops all this yelling of his and he asks me, 'What's so funny?' Can you believe it? Like he wants me to explain the joke to him so he can laugh, too. 'What's so funny?' "

I poured the rest of my bourbon into my coffee and stirred it with a spoon. I was getting bits and pieces of Richard Vanderpoel. So far they didn't begin to fit together, but they were fragments of what might ultimately be a full picture. Or they might never add up to anything real. Sometimes the whole is a lot less than the sum of its parts.

I spent another twenty minutes or so with Pankow, going back and forth over places we'd already been without getting anything much from him. He talked a little about his reactions to the murder scene, the nausea, the hysteria. He wanted to know if you ever got used to that sort of thing. I thought of the photograph I had taken from the file. I hadn't felt much looking at it. But if I had walked into that bedroom as Pankow had done, I might have reacted in very much the same way.

"You get used to some of it," I told him, "but every once in a while something new comes along and knocks you on your ass."

When I had all I was going to get, I put a five on the table for the drinks and passed him twenty-five dollars. He didn't want to take it.

"C'mon," I said. "You did me a favor."

"Well, that's all it was, was a favor. I feel funny taking money for it."

"You're being stupid."

"Huh?" The blue eyes were very wide.

"Stupid. This isn't graft. It's clean money. You did somebody a favor and made a couple of bucks for it." I pushed the bills across the table at him. "Listen to me," I said. "You just made a good collar. You wrote a decent report, and you handle yourself well, and pretty soon you'll be in line to get off the beat and into a prowl car. But nobody's going to want you in a car with him if you've got the wrong kind of reputation."

"I don't get you."

"Think about it. If you don't take money when somebody puts it in your hand, you're going to make a lot of people very nervous. You don't have to be a crook. Certain kinds of money you can turn down. And you don't have to walk the streets with your hand out. But you've got to play the game with the cards they give you. Take the money."

"Jesus."

"Didn't Koehler tell you there would be something in it for you?"

"Sure. But that's not why I came here. Hell, I generally drop in for a couple of beers when my shift ends. I usually meet my girl here around ten thirty. It's not like—"

"Koehler's going to expect a five-dollar bill for

steering twenty-five your way. You want to pay him out of your own pocket?''

"Jesus. What do I do, just walk into his office and hand him five dollars?''

"That's the idea. You can say something like, 'Here's that five you loaned me.' Something like that.''

"I guess I got a lot to learn," he said. He didn't sound delighted at the prospect.

"You don't have to worry about it," I said. "You've got plenty to learn, but they make it easy for you. The system takes you through it a step at a time. That's what makes it such a good system.''

He insisted on buying me a drink out of his new-found wealth. I sat there and drank it while he told me what it meant to him to be a police officer. I nodded at the right times without paying very much attention to what he was saying. I couldn't keep my mind on his words.

I got out of there and walked crosstown on Fifty-seventh to my hotel. The early edition of the *Times* was just in at the newsstand on Eighth Avenue. I bought it and took it home with me.

There were no messages for me at the desk. I went up to my room and took my shoes off and stretched out on the bed with the paper. It turned out to be about as gripping as Lewis Pankow's conversation.

I got undressed. When I took off my shirt, the photo of Wendy Hanniford's dead body fell onto the floor. I picked it up and looked at it and imagined myself as Lewis Pankow, walking in on a scene like that with the killer manacled to my wrist, then hauling him across the room so that I

could vomit in the corner, then giggling hysterically until Richard Vanderpoel quite reasonably
asked the cause of my mirth.

"What's so funny?"

I took a shower and put my clothes back on
again. It had been snowing hesitantly earlier, and
now it was beginning to accumulate. I walked
around the corner to Armstrong's and took a
stool at the bar.

He lived with her like brother and sister. He
killed her and shrieked that he had fucked his
mother. He rushed out into the street covered with
her blood.

I knew too few facts, and the ones I did know
did not seem to fit together.

I drank a few drinks and sidestepped a few con-
versations. I looked around for Trina, but she had
left when her shift ended. I let the bartender tell
me what was the matter with the Knicks this year.
I don't remember what he said, just that he felt
very strongly about it.

FIVE

Gordon Kalish had an old-fashioned pendulum clock on his wall, the kind that used to hang in railway stations. He kept glancing at it and checking the time against his wristwatch. At first I thought he was trying to tell me something. Later I realized it was a habit. Early in life someone must have told him his time was valuable. He had never forgotten, but he still couldn't entirely make himself believe it.

He was a partner in Bowdoin Realty Management. I had arrived at the company's offices in the Flatiron Building a few minutes after ten and waited for about twenty minutes until Kalish could give me a chunk of his time. Now he had papers and ledgers spread out on his desk and was apologetic that he couldn't be more helpful.

"We rented the apartment to Miss Hanniford herself," he said. "She may have had a roommate from the beginning. If so, she didn't tell us about it. She was the tenant of record. She could have had anyone living with her, man or woman, and we wouldn't have known about it. Or cared."

"She had a female roommate when Miss Antonelli moved in as superintendent. I'd like to contact that woman."

"I have no way of knowing who she was. Or when she moved in or out. As long as Miss Hanniford came up with the rent the first of every month, and as long as she didn't create a nuisance, we had no reason to take any further interest." He scratched his head. "If there was another woman and she moved out, wouldn't the post office have a forwarding address?"

"I'd need her name to get it."

"Oh, of course." His eyes went to the clock, then to his watch, then again to me. "It was a very different matter when my father first got into the business. He ran things on a much more personal basis. He was a plumber originally. He saved his money and bought property, a building at a time. Did all his own repair work, put the profits from one building into the acquisition of another. And he knew his tenants. He went around to collect the rent in person. The first of the month, or once a week in some of the buildings. He would carry certain tenants for months if they were going through hard times. Others he had out on the street if they were five days late. He said you had to be a good judge of people."

"He must have been quite a man."

"He still is. He's retired now, of course. He's been living down in Florida for five or six years now. Picks oranges off his own trees. And still pays his dues in the plumbers union every year." He clasped his hands together. "It's a different business now. We've sold off most of the buildings he bought. Ownership is too much of a headache. It's a lot less grief to manage property for somebody else. The building where Miss Hanniford lived, 194 Bethune, the owner is a housewife in a suburb of Chicago who inherited the property from an uncle. She's never seen it, just gets her check from us four times a year.''

I said, ''Miss Hanniford was a model tenant, then?''

''In that she never did anything to draw our attention. The papers say she was a prostitute. Could be, I suppose. We never had any complaints.''

''You never met her?''

''No.''

''She was always on time with the rent?''

''She was a week late now and then, just like everybody. No more than that.''

''She paid by check?''

''Yes.''

''When did she sign the lease?''

''What did I do with the lease? Here it is. Let's see, now. October 23, 1970. Standard two-year lease, renewing automatically.''

''And the monthly rent was four hundred dollars?''

''It's three eighty-five now. It was lower then, there've been some allowable increases since then. It was three forty-two fifty when she signed it.''

''You wouldn't rent to someone with no visible means of support.''

''Of course not.''

''Then she must have claimed to be working. She must have provided references.''

''I should have thought of that,'' he said. He shuffled more papers and came up with the application she had filled out. I looked at it. She had claimed to be employed as an industrial systems analyst at a salary of seventeen thousand dollars a year. Her employer was one J.J. Cottrell, Inc. There was a telephone number listed, and I copied it down.

I asked if the references had been checked.

"They must have been," Kalish said. "But it doesn't amount to anything. It's simple enough to fake. All she needs is someone at that number to back up her story. We make the calls automatically, but I sometimes wonder if it's worth the trouble."

"Then someone must have called this number. And someone answered the phone and swore to her lies."

"Evidently."

I thanked him for his time. In the lobby downstairs I put a dime in a pay phone and dialed the number Wendy had given. A recording informed me that the number I had dialed was no longer in service.

I put my dime back in the phone and called the Carlyle. I asked the desk for Cale Hanniford's room. A woman answered the phone on the second ring. I gave my name and asked to speak to Mr. Hanniford. He asked me if I was making any progress.

"I don't know," I said. "Those postcards you received from Wendy. Do you still have them?"

"It's possible. Is it important?"

"It would help me get the chronology in order. She signed the lease on her apartment three years ago in October. You said she dropped out of college in the spring."

"I believe it was in March."

"When did you get the first postcard?"

"Within two or three months, as I remember it.

Let me ask my wife." He was back a moment later. "My wife says the first card arrived in June. I would have said late May. The second card, the one from Florida, was a few months after that. I'm sorry I can't make it more specific than that. My wife says she thinks she remembers where she put the cards. We'll be returning to Utica tomorrow morning. I gather you want to know whether Wendy went to Florida before or after she took the apartment."

That was close enough, so I said yes. I told him I'd call him in a day or two. I already had his office number in Utica, and he gave me his home number as well. "But please try to call me at the office," he said.

Burghash Antiques Imports was on University Place between Eleventh and Twelfth. I stood in one aisle surrounded by the residue of half the attics in Western Europe. I was looking at a clock just like the one I had seen on Gordon Kalish's wall. It was priced at $225.

"Are you interested in clocks? That's a good one."

"Does it keep time?"

"Oh, those pendulum clocks are indestructible. And they're extraordinarily accurate. You just raise or lower the weight to make them run faster or slower. The case of the one you're looking at is in particularly good condition. It's not a rare model, of course, but they're hard to find in such nice shape. The price might be somewhat negotiable if you're really interested."

I turned to take a good look at him. He was in his middle or late twenties, a trim young man wearing flannel slacks and a powder-blue turtleneck sweater. His hair had been expensively styled. His sideburns were even with the bottoms of his earlobes. He had a very precise moustache.

I said, "Actually, I'm not interested in clocks. I wanted to talk to someone about a boy who used to work here."

"Oh, you must mean Richie! You're a policeman? Wasn't it the most unbelievable thing?"

"Did you know him well?"

"I hardly knew him at all. I've only been here since just before Thanksgiving. I used to work at the auction gallery down the block, but it was terribly hectic."

"How long had Richie worked here?"

"I don't honestly know. Mr. Burghash could tell you. He's in back in the office. It has been pure hell for all of us since that happened. I still can't believe it."

"Were you working here the day it happened?"

He nodded. "I saw him that morning. Thursday morning. Then I was on a delivery all afternoon, a load of perfectly hideous French country furniture for an equally hideous split-level chateau in Syosset. That's on Long Island."

"I know."

"Well, *I* didn't. I lived all these many years in blissful ignorance that there even *was* a place known as Syosset." He remembered the gravity of what we were talking about, and his face turned serious again. "I got back here at five, just in time to help close up shop. Richie had left early. Of course by then it had all happened, hadn't it?"

"The murder took place around four."

"While I was fighting traffic on the Long Island Expressway." He shivered theatrically. "I had no idea until I caught the eleven o'clock news that

43

night. And I couldn't believe it was our Richard Vanderpoel, but they mentioned the name of the firm and—'' He sighed and let his hands drop to his sides. "One never knows," he said.

"What was he like?"

"I hardly had time to know him. He was pleasant, he was courteous, he was anxious to please. He didn't have a great *knowledge* of antiques, but he had a good *sense* of them if you know what I mean."

"Did you know he was living with a girl?"

"How would I have known that?"

"He might have mentioned it."

"Well, he didn't. Why?"

"Does it surprise you that he was living with a girl?"

"I'm sure I never thought about it one way or the other."

"Was he homosexual?"

"How on earth would *I* know?"

I stepped closer to him. He backed away without moving his feet. I said, "Why don't you cut the shit."

"Pardon me?"

"Was Richie gay?"

"I certainly had no interest in him myself. And I never saw him with another man, and he never seemed to be cruising anyone."

"Did you think he was gay?"

"Well, I always assumed it, for heaven's sake. He certainly *seemed* gay."

I found Burghash in the office. He was a little man with a furrowed brow that went almost to the top of his head. He had a ragged moustache and two days' worth of beard. He told me he'd had cops and newspapermen coming out of his ears and he had a business to run. I told him I wouldn't take much of his time.

"I have a few questions," I said. "Let's go back to Thursday, the day of the murder. Did Richie behave differently than usual?"

"Not really."

"He wasn't agitated or anything like that?"

"No."

"He went home early."

"That's right. He didn't feel well when he came back from lunch. He had some curry at the Indian place around the corner, and it didn't agree with him. I was always telling him to stay with bland food, ordinary American food. He had a sensitive digestive system, and he was always trying exotic foods that didn't agree with him."

"What time did he leave here?"

"I don't keep track. He came back from lunch feeling lousy. I told him right away to take the rest of the day off. You can't work with your guts on fire. He wanted to tough it out, though. He was an ambitious kid, a hard worker. Sometimes he'd have indigestion like that, and then an hour later he'd be all right again, but this time it got worse instead of better, and I finally told him to get the hell out and go home. He must have left here, oh, I don't know. Three? Three thirty? Something like that."

"How long had he been working for you?"

"Just about a year and a half. He went to work for me a year ago last July."

"He moved in with Wendy Hanniford the following December. Did you have a previous address for him?"

"The YMCA on Twenty-third Street. That's

where he was living when he came to work for me. Then he moved a few times. I don't have the addresses, and then I guess it was in December when he moved to Bethune Street.''

"Did you know anything about Wendy Hanniford?"

He shook his head. "Never met her. Never knew her name.''

"You knew he was rooming with a girl?"

"I knew he said he was.''

"Oh?''

Burghash shrugged. "I figured he was rooming with somebody, and if he wanted me to think it was a girl, I was willing to go along with it.''

"You thought he was homosexual.''

"Uh-huh. It's not exactly unheard of in this business. I don't care if my employees go to bed with orangutans. What they do on their own time is their own business.''

"Did he have any friends that you knew of?"

"Not that I knew of, no. He kept to himself most of the time.''

"And he was a good worker.''

"Very good. Very conscientious, and he had a feeling for the business.'' He fixed his eyes on the ceiling. "I sensed that he had personal problems. He never talked about them, but he was, oh, how shall I put it? High-strung.''

"Nervous? Touchy?"

"No, not that, exactly. High-strung is the best adjective I can think of to describe him. You sensed that he had things weighing him down, keying him up. But you know, that was more noticeable when he first started here. For the past year he seemed more settled, as if he had managed to come to terms with himself.''

"The past year. Since he moved in with the Hanniford girl, in other words."

"I hadn't thought of it that way, but I guess that's right."

"You were surprised when he killed her."

"I was astonished. I simply could not believe it. And I'm still astonished. You see someone five days a week for a year and a half, and you think you know them. Then you find out you don't know them at all."

On my way out the young man in the turtleneck stopped me. He asked me if I had learned anything useful. I told him I didn't know.

"But it's all over," he said. "Isn't it? They're both dead."

"Yes."

"So what's the point in poking around in corners?"

"I have no idea," I said. "Why do you suppose he was living with her?"

"Why does anybody live with anybody else?"

"Let's assume he was gay. Why would he live with a woman?"

"Maybe he got tired of dusting and cleaning. Sick of doing his own laundry."

"I don't know that she was that domestic. It seems likely that she was a prostitute."

"So I understand."

"Why would a homosexual live with a prostitute?"

"Gawd, *I* don't know. Maybe she let him take care of her overflow. Maybe he was a closet heterosexual. For my own part, I'd never live with anyone, male *or* female. I have trouble enough living with myself."

I couldn't argue with that. I started toward the

door, then turned around again. There were too many things that didn't fit together, and they were scraping against each other like chalk on a blackboard. "I just want to make sense out of this," I said, to myself as much as to him. "Why in hell would he kill her? He raped her and he killed her. Why?"

"Well, he was a minister's son."

"So?"

"They're all crazy," he said. "Aren't they?"

SIX

The Reverend Martin Vanderpoel didn't want to see me. "I have spoken with enough reporters," he told me. "I can spare no time for you, Mr. Scudder. I have my responsibilities to my congregation. What time remains, I feel the need to devote to prayer and meditation."

I knew the feeling. I explained that I wasn't a reporter, that I was representing Cole Hanniford, the father of the murdered girl.

"I see," he said.

"I wouldn't need much of your time, Reverend Vanderpoel. Mr. Hanniford has suffered a loss, even as you have. In a sense, he lost his daughter before she was killed. Now he wants to learn more about her."

"I'd be a poor source of information, I'm afraid."

"He told me he wanted to see you himself, sir."

There was a long pause. I thought for a moment that the phone had gone dead. Then he said, "It is a difficult request to refuse. I will be occupied with church affairs this afternoon, I'm afraid. Perhaps this evening?"

"This evening would be fine."

"You have the address of the church? The rectory is adjacent to it. I will be waiting for you at—shall we say eight o'clock?"

I said eight would be fine. I found another dime and looked up another number and made a call, and the man I spoke to was a good deal less reticent to talk about Richard Vanderpoel. In fact he seemed relieved that I'd called him and told me to come right on up.

His name was George Topakian, and he and his brother constituted Topakian and Topakian, Attorneys-at-Law. His office was on Madison Avenue in the low Forties. Framed diplomas on the wall testified that he had graduated from City College twenty-two years ago and had then gone on to Fordham Law.

He was a small man, trimly built, dark complected. He seated me in a red leather tub chair and asked me if I wanted coffee. I said coffee would be fine. He buzzed his secretary on the intercom and had her bring a cup for each of us. While she was doing this, he told me he and his brother had a general practice with an emphasis on estate work. The only criminal cases he'd handled, aside from minor work for regular clients, had come as a result of court assignments. Most of these had involved minor offenses—purse snatching, low-level assault, possession of narcotics—until the court had appointed him as counsel to Richard Vanderpoel.

"I expected to be relieved," he said. "His father was a clergyman and would almost certainly have arranged my replacement by a criminal lawyer. But I did see Vanderpoel.''

"When did you see him?"

"Late Friday afternoon." He scratched the side of his nose with his index finger. "I could have gotten to him earlier, I guess."

"But you didn't."

"No. I stalled." He looked at me levelly. "I was anticipating being replaced," he said. "And if replacement was imminent, I thought I could save myself the time I'd spend seeing him. And my time wasn't the half of it."

"How do you mean?"

"I didn't want to see the son of a bitch."

He got up from behind his desk and walked over to the window. He toyed with the cord of the venetian blinds, raising and lowering them a few inches. I waited him out. He sighed and turned to face me.

"Here was a guy who committed a horrible murder, slashed a young woman to death. I didn't want to set eyes on him. Do you find that hard to understand?"

"Not at all."

"It bothered me. I'm an attorney, I'm supposed to represent people without regard to what they have or haven't done. I should have thrown myself right into it, finding the best defense for him. I certainly shouldn't have presumed my own client guilty as charged without even talking to him." He came back to his desk and sat down again. "But of course I did. The police picked him up right on the scene of the crime. I might have challenged their case if I saw it all the way into court, but in my own mind I had already tried the bastard and found him guilty as charged. And since I had every expectation that I would be taken off the case, I found ways to avoid seeing Vanderpoel."

"But you eventually went that Friday afternoon."

"Uh-huh. He was in his cell in the Tombs."

"You saw him in his cell, then."

"Yes. I didn't pay much attention to the surroundings. They've finally torn down the Women's House of Detention. I used to walk past it all the time years ago when my wife and I lived in the Village. A horrible place."

"I know."

"I wish they'd do the same for the Tombs." He touched the side of his nose again. "I suppose I saw the very steam pipe that poor bastard hanged himself from. And the bedsheet he used to do the job. He sat on his bed while we talked. He let me have the chair."

"How long were you with him?"

"I don't think it was more than half an hour. It seemed considerably longer."

"Did he talk?"

"Not at first. He was off somewhere with his own thoughts. I tried to get through to him but didn't have very much luck. He had a look in his eyes as if he was having some intense wordless dialogue with himself. I tried to open him up, and at the same time I began planning the defense I would use if I had the chance. I didn't expect to have the chance, understand. It was a hypothetical exercise as far as I was concerned. But I had more or less decided to try for an insanity plea."

"Everyone seems to agree he was crazy."

"There's a difference between that and legal insanity. It becomes a battle of experts—you line up your witnesses, and the prosecution lines up theirs. Well, I went on talking to him, just trying to get him to open up a little, and then he turned to me and looked at me as if wondering where I had come from, as if he hadn't known I was in the room before. He asked me who I was, and I went over everything I had said to him the first time around.''

"Did he seem rational?''

Topakian considered the question. "I don't know that he seemed to *be* rational,'' he said. "He seemed to be *acting* rationally at that moment.''

"What did he say?''

"I wish I could remember it exactly. I asked him if he had killed the Hanniford girl. He said, now let me think, he said, 'She couldn't have done it herself.' ''

" 'She couldn't have done it herself.' ''

"I think that's the way he put it. I asked if he remembered killing her. He claimed that he didn't. He said his stomach ached, and at first I thought he meant he had a stomachache at the time of our conversation, but I gathered that he had had a stomachache on the day of the murder.''

"He left work early because of indigestion.''

"Well, he remembered the stomachache. He said his stomach ached and he went to the apartment. Then he kept talking about blood. 'She was in the bathtub and there was blood all over.' I understand they found her in bed.''

"Yes.''

"She hadn't been in the tub or anything?''

"She was killed in bed, according to police reports.''

He shook his head. "He was a very confused

53

young man. He said that she had been in the tub with blood everywhere. I asked him if he had killed her, I asked him several times, and he never really gave me an answer. Sometimes he said that he didn't remember killing her. Other times he said that he must have killed her because she couldn't have done it herself.''

"He said that more than once, then.''

"Quite a few times.''

"That's interesting.''

"Is it?'' Topakian shrugged. "I don't think he ever lied to me. I mean, I don't believe he remembered killing the girl. Because he admitted something, oh, worse.''

"What?''

"Having sex with her.''

"That's worse than killing her?''

"Having sex with her afterward.''

"Oh.''

"He didn't make any attempt to conceal it. He said he found her lying in her blood and he had sex with her.''

"What words did he use?''

"I don't know exactly. You mean for the sex act? He said he fucked her.''

"After she was dead.''

"Evidently.''

"And he had no trouble remembering that?''

"None. I don't know whether he had sex with her before or after the murder. Did the autopsy indicate anything one way or the other?''

"If it did, it wasn't in the report. I'm not sure they can tell if the two acts are close together in time. Why?''

"I don't know. He kept saying, 'I fucked her and she's dead.' As if his having had sex with her

54

was the chief cause of her death.''

"But he never remembered killing her. I suppose he could have blocked it out easily enough. I wonder why he didn't block out the whole thing. The sex act. Let me go over this once more. He said he walked in and found her like that?''

"I can't remember everything all that clearly myself, Scudder. He walked in and she was dead in the tub, that's what he said. He didn't even say specifically that she was dead, just that she was in a tub full of blood.''

"Did you ask him about the murder weapon?''

"I asked him what he did with it.''

"And?''

"He didn't know.''

"Did you ask him what the murder weapon was?''

"No. I didn't have to. He said, 'I don't know what happened to the razor.' ''

"He knew it was a razor?''

"Evidently. Why wouldn't he know?''

"Well, if he didn't remember having it in his hand, why should he remember what it was?''

"Maybe he heard someone talk about the murder weapon and speak of it as a razor.''

"Maybe,'' I said.

I walked for a while, heading generally south and west. I stopped for a drink on Sixth Avenue around Thirty-seventh Street. A man a couple of stools down was telling the bartender that he was sick of working his ass off to buy Cadillacs for niggers on welfare. The bartender said, "You? Chrissake, you're in here eight hours a day. The taxes you pay, they don't get more'n a hubcap out of you.''

A little farther south and west I went into a church and sat for a while. St. John's, I think it was. I sat near the front and watched people go in and out of the confessional. They didn't look any different coming out than they had going in. I thought how nice it might be to be able to leave your sins in a little curtained booth.

Richie Vanderpoel and Wendy Hanniford, and I kept picking at threads and trying to find a pattern to them. There was a conclusion I kept feeling myself drawn toward, and I didn't want to take hold of it. It was wrong, it had to be wrong, and as long as it reached out, tantalizing me, it kept me from doing the job I had signed on for.

I knew what had to come next. I had been ducking it, but it kept waving at me and I couldn't duck it forever. And now was the best time of day for it. Much better than trying it in the middle of the night.

I hung around long enough to light a couple of candles and stuff a few bills in the offerings slot. Then I caught a cab in front of Penn Station and told the driver how to get to Bethune Street.

The first-floor tenants were out. A Mrs. Hacker on the second floor said she had had very little contact with Wendy and Richard. She remembered that Wendy's former roommate had had dark hair. Sometimes, she said, they had played their radio or stereo loud at night, but it had never been bad enough to complain about. She liked music, she said. She liked all kinds of music, classical, semiclassical, popular—all kinds of music.

The door to the third-floor apartment had a padlock on it. It would have been easy enough to crack it but impossible to do so unobtrusively.

There was nobody home on the fourth floor. I was very glad of that. I went on up to the fifth floor. Elizabeth Antonelli had said the tenants wouldn't be back until March. I rang their bell and listened carefully for sounds within the apartment. I didn't hear any.

There were four locks on the door, including a Taylor that is as close as you can come to pick-proof. I knocked off the other three with a celluloid strip, an old oil-company credit card that is otherwise useless since I no longer own a car. Then I kicked the Taylor in. I had to kick it twice before the door flew inward.

I locked the other three locks after me. The tenants would have a lot of fun trying to figure out what had happened to the Taylor, but that was their problem, and it wouldn't come up until sometime in March. I poked until I found the window that fed onto the fire escape, opened it, and climbed down two stories to the Hanniford-Vanderpoel apartment.

The window wasn't locked. I opened it, let myself in, closed it after me.

An hour later I went out the window and back up the fire escape. There were lights on in the fourth-floor apartment by now, but the shade was drawn on the window I had to pass. I reentered the fifth-floor apartment, let myself out into the hallway, locked the door behind me, and went downstairs and out of the building. I had enough time to grab a sandwich before I kept my appointment with Martin Vanderpoel.

SEVEN

I got off the BMT at Sixty-second Street and New Utrecht and walked a couple of blocks through a part of Brooklyn where Bay Ridge and Bensonhurst rub shoulders with one another. A powdery rain was melting some of yesterday's snow. The weather bureau expected it to freeze sometime during the night. I was a little early and stopped at a drugstore lunch counter for a cup of coffee. Toward the rear of the counter a kid was demonstrating a gravity knife to a couple of his friends. He took a quick look at me and made the knife disappear, reminding me once again that I haven't stopped looking like a cop.

I drank half my coffee and walked the rest of the way to the church. It was a massive edifice of white stone toned all shades of gray by the years. A cornerstone announced that the present structure had been erected in 1886 by a congregation established 220 years before that date. An illuminated bulletin board identified the church as the First Reformed Church of Bay Ridge, Reverend Martin T. Vanderpoel, Pastor. Services were held

Sundays at nine thirty; this coming Sunday Reverend Vanderpoel was slated to speak on "The Road to Hell Is Paved with Good Intentions."

I turned the corner and found the rectory immediately adjacent to the church. It was three stories tall and built of the same distinctive stone. I rang the bell and stood on the front step in the rain for a few minutes. Then a small gray-haired woman opened the door and peered up at me. I gave my name.

"Yes," she said. "He said he was expecting you." She led me into a parlor and pointed me to an armchair. I sat down across from a fireplace with an electric fire glowing in it. The wall on either side of the fireplace was lined with bookshelves. An Oriental rug with a muted pattern covered most of the parquet floor. The room's furniture was all dark and massive. I sat there waiting for him and decided I should have stopped for a drink instead of a cup of coffee. I wasn't likely to get a drink in this cheerless house.

He let me sit there for five minutes. Then I heard his step on the stairs. I got to my feet as he entered the room. He said, "Mr. Scudder? I'm sorry to keep you waiting. I was on the telephone. But please have a seat, won't you?"

He was very tall and rail-thin. He wore a plain black suit, a clerical collar, and a pair of black leather bedroom slippers. His hair was white with yellow highlights here and there. It would have been considered long a few years ago, but now the abundant curls were conservative enough. His horn-rimmed glasses had thick lenses that made it difficult for me to see his eyes.

"Coffee, Mr. Scudder?"

"No, thank you."

"And none for me, either. If I have more than one cup with my dinner, I'm up half the night." He sat down in a chair that was a mate to mine. He leaned toward me and placed his hands on his knees. "Well, now," he said. "I don't see how I can possibly help you, but please tell me if I can."

I explained a little more fully the errand I was running for Cale Hanniford. When I had finished he touched his chin with his thumb and forefinger and nodded thoughtfully.

"Mr. Hanniford has lost a daughter," he said. "And I have lost a son."

"Yes."

"It's so difficult to father children in today's world, Mr. Scudder. Perhaps it was always thus, but it seems to me that the times conspire against us. Oh, I can sympathize fully with Mr. Hanniford, more fully than ever since I have suffered a similar loss." He turned to gaze at the fire. "But I fear I have no sympathy for the girl."

I didn't say anything.

"It's a failing on my part, and I recognize it as such. Man is an imperfect creature. Sometimes it seems to me that religion has no higher function than to sharpen his awareness of the extent of his imperfection. God alone is perfect. Even Man, His greatest handiwork, is hopelessly flawed. A paradox, Mr. Scudder, don't you think?"

"Yes."

"Not the least of my own flaws is an inability to grieve for Wendy Hanniford. You see, her father no doubt holds my son responsible for the loss of his daughter. And I, in turn, hold his daughter responsible for the loss of my son."

He got to his feet and approached the fireplace. He stood there for a moment, his back perfectly straight, warming his hands. He turned toward me and seemed on the point of saying something. Instead, he walked slowly to his chair and sat down again, this time crossing one leg over the other.

He said, "Are you a Christian, Mr. Scudder?"

"No."

"A Jew?"

"I have no religion."

"How sad for you," he said. "I asked your religion because the nature of your own beliefs might facilitate your understanding my feelings toward the Hanniford girl. But perhaps I can approach the matter in another way. Do you believe in good and evil, Mr. Scudder?"

"Yes, I do."

"Do you believe that there is such a thing as evil extant in the world?"

"I know there is."

He nodded, satisfied. "So do I," he said. "It would be difficult to believe otherwise, whatever one's religious outlook. A glance at a daily newspaper provides evidence enough of the existence of evil." He paused, and I thought he was waiting for me to say something. Then he said, "*She* was evil."

"Wendy Hanniford?"

"Yes. An evil, Devil-ridden woman. She took my son away from me, away from his religion, away from God. She led him away from good paths and unto the paths of evil." His voice was picking up a timbre, and I could imagine his forcefulness in front of a congregation. "It was my son who killed her. But it was she who killed something within him, who made it possible for him to kill." His voice dropped in pitch, and he held his hands palms down at his sides. "And so I cannot mourn Wendy Hanniford. I can regret that her death came at Richard's hands, I can profoundly regret that he then took his own life, but I cannot mourn your client's daughter.''

He let his hands drop, lowered his head. I couldn't see his eyes, but his face was troubled, wrapped up in chains of good and evil. I thought of the sermon he would preach on Sunday, thought of all the different roads to Hell and all the paving stones therein. I pictured Martin Vanderpoel as a long, lean Sisyphus arduously rolling the boulders into place.

I said, ''Your son was in Manhattan a year and a half ago. That was when he went to work for Burghash Antiques.'' He nodded. ''So he left here some six months before he began sharing Wendy Hanniford's apartment.''

''That is correct.''

''But you feel she led him astray.''

''Yes.'' He took a deep breath and let it out slowly. ''My son left my home shortly after his high school graduation. I did not approve, but neither did I object violently. I would have wanted Richard to go to college. He was an intelligent boy and would have done well in college. I had hopes, naturally enough, that he might follow me into the ministry. I did not force him in this direction, however. One must determine for oneself whether one has a vocation. I am not fanatical on the subject, Mr. Scudder. I would prefer to see a son of mine as a contented and productive doctor or lawyer or businessman than as a discontented minister of the gospel.

''I realized that Richard had to find himself. That's a fashionable term with the young these days, is it not? He had to find himself. I understood this. I expected that this process of self-discovery would ultimately lead him to enter college after a year or two. I hoped this would occur, but in any event I saw no cause for alarm. Richard had an honest job, he was living in a decent Christian residence, and I felt that his feet were on a good path. Not perhaps the path he would ultimately pursue, but one that was correct for him at that point in his life.

"Then he met Wendy Hanniford. He lived in sin with her. He became corrupted by her. And, ultimately—"

I remembered a bit of men's-room graffiti: *Happiness is when your son marries a boy of his own faith.* Evidently Richie Vanderpoel had functioned as some variety of homosexual without his father ever suspecting anything. Then he moved in with a girl, and his father was shattered.

I said, "Reverend Vanderpoel, a great many young people live together nowadays without being married."

"I recognize this, Mr. Scudder. I do not condone it, but I could hardly fail to recognize it."

"But your feeling in this case was more than a matter of not condoning it."

"Yes."

"Why?"

"Because Wendy Hanniford was evil."

I was getting the first twinges of a headache. I rubbed the center of my forehead with the tips of my fingers. I said, "What I want more than anything else is to be able to give her father a picture of her. You say she was evil. In what way was she evil?"

"She was an older woman who enticed an innocent young man into an unnatural relationship."

"She was only three or four years older than Richard."

"Yes, I know. In chronological terms. In terms of worldliness she was ages his senior. She was promiscuous. She was amoral. She was a creature of perversion."

"Did you ever actually meet her?"

"Yes," he said. He breathed in and out. "I met her once. Once was enough."

"When did that take place?"

"It's hard for me to remember. I believe it was during the spring. April or May, I would say."

"Did he bring her here?"

"No. No, Richard surely knew better than to bring that woman into my house. I went to the apartment where they were living. I went specifically to meet with her, to talk to her. I picked a time when Richard would be working at his job."

"And you met Wendy."

"I did."

"What did you hope to accomplish?"

"I wanted her to end her relationship with my son."

"And she refused."

"Oh, yes, Mr. Scudder. She refused." He leaned back in his chair, closed his eyes. "She was foulmouthed and abusive. She taunted me. She—I don't want to go into this further, Mr. Scudder. She made it quite clear that she had no intention of giving Richard up. It suited her to have him living with her. The entire interview was one of the most unpleasant experiences of my life."

"And you never saw her again."

"I did not. I saw Richard on several occasions, but not in that apartment. I tried to talk to him about that woman. I made no progress whatsoever. He was utterly infatuated with her. Sex—evil, unscrupulous sex—gives certain women an extraordinary hold upon susceptible men. Man is a weakling, Mr. Scudder, and he is so often powerless to cope with the awful force of an evil woman's sexuality." He sighed heavily. "And in the end she was destroyed by means of her own evil nature. The sexual spell she cast upon my son was the instrument of her own undoing."

"You make her sound like a witch."

He smiled slightly. "A witch? Indeed I do. A less enlightened generation than our own would have seen her burned at the stake for witchcraft. Nowadays we speak of neuroses, of psychological complications, of compulsion. Previously we spoke of witchcraft, of demonic possession. I wonder sometimes if we're as enlightened now as we prefer to think. Or if our enlightenment does us much good."

"Does anything?"

"Pardon?"

"I was wondering if anything did us much good."

"Ah," he said. He took off his glasses and perched them on his knee. I hadn't seen the color of his eyes before. They were a light blue flecked with gold. He said, "You have no faith, Mr. Scudder. Perhaps that accounts for your cynicism."

"Perhaps."

"I would say that God's love does us a great deal of good. In the next world if not in this one."

I decided I would rather deal with one world at a time. I asked if Richie had had faith.

"He was in a period of doubt. He was too preoccupied with his attempt at self-realization to have room for the realization of the Lord."

"I see."

"And then he fell under the spell of the Hanniford woman. I use the word advisedly. He literally fell under her spell."

"What was he like before that?"

"A good boy. An aware, interested, involved young man."

"You never had any problems with him?"

"No problems." He put his glasses back on. "I cannot avoid blaming myself, Mr. Scudder."

"For what?"

"For everything. What is it that they say? 'The cobbler's children always go barefoot.' Perhaps that maxim applies in this case. Perhaps I devoted too much attention to my congregation and too little attention to my son. I had to raise him by myself, you see. That did not seem a difficult chore at the time. It may have been more difficult than I ever realized."

"Richard's mother—"

He closed his eyes. "I lost my wife almost fifteen years ago," he said.

"I didn't know that."

"It was hard for both of us. For Richard and for myself. In retrospect I think that I should have married again. I never . . . never entertained the idea. I was able to have a housekeeper, and my own duties facilitated my spending more time with him than the average father might have been able to manage. I thought that was sufficient."

"And now you don't think so?"

"I don't know. I occasionally think there is very little we can do to change our destiny. Our lives play themselves out according to a master plan." He smiled briefly. "That is either a very comforting thing to believe or quite the opposite, Mr. Scudder."

"I can see how it could be."

"Other times I think there ought to have been something I could have done. Richard was drawn very much into himself. He was shy, reticent, very much a private person."

"Did he have much of a social life? I mean during high school, while he was living here."

"He had friends."

"Did he date?"

"He wasn't interested in girls at that time. He was never interested in girls until he came into that woman's clutches."

"Did it bother you that he wasn't interested in girls?"

That was as close as I cared to come to intimating that Richie was interested in boys instead. If it registered at all, Vanderpoel didn't show it. "I was not concerned," he said. "I took it for granted that Richard would ultimately develop a fine and healthy loving relationship with the girl who would eventually become his wife and bear his children. That he was not involved in social dating in the meantime did not upset me. If you were in a position to see what I see, Mr. Scudder, you would realize that a great deal of trouble stems from too much involvement of one sex with the other sex. I have seen girls pregnant in their early teens. I have seen young men forced into marriage at a very tender age. I have seen young people afflicted with unmentionable diseases. No, I was if anything delighted that Richard was a late bloomer in this area."

He shook his head. "And yet," he said, "perhaps if he had been more experienced, perhaps if he had been less innocent, he would not have been so easy a victim for Miss Hanniford."

We sat for a few moments in silence. I asked him a few more things without getting anything significant in reply. He asked again if I wanted a cup of coffee. I declined and said it was time I was getting on my way. He didn't try to persuade me to stay.

I got my coat from the vestibule closet where the housekeeper had stashed it. As I was putting it on I said, "I understand you saw your son once after the killing."

"Yes."

"In his cell."

"That is correct." He winced almost imperceptibly at the recollection. "We didn't speak at length. I tried only to do what little I could to put his mind at rest. Evidently I failed. He . . . he elected to mete out his own punishment for what he had done."

"I talked to the lawyer his case was assigned to. A Mr. Topakian."

"I didn't meet the man myself. After Richard . . . took his own life . . . well, I saw no point in seeing the lawyer. And I couldn't bring myself to do it."

"I understand." I finished buttoning my coat. "Topakian said Richard had no memory of the actual murder."

"Oh?"

"Did your son say anything to you about it?"

He hesitated for a moment, and I didn't think he was going to answer. Then he gave his head an impatient shake. "There's no harm in saying it now, is there? Perhaps he was speaking truthfully to the lawyer, perhaps his memory was clouded at the time.'' He sighed again. ''Richard told me he had killed her. He said he did not know what had come over him.''

''Did he give any explanation?''

''Explanation? I don't know if you would call it an explanation, Mr. Scudder. It explained certain things to me, however.''

''What did he say?''

He looked off over my shoulder, searching his mind for the right words. Finally he said, ''He told me that there was a sudden moment of awful clarity when he saw her face. He said it was as if he had been given a glimpse of the Devil and knew only that he must destroy, destroy.''

''I see.''

''Without absolving my son, Mr. Scudder, I nevertheless hold Miss Hanniford responsible for the loss of her own life. She snared him, she blinded him to her real self, and then for a moment the veil slipped aside, the blindfold was loosed from around his eyes, and he saw her plain. And saw, I feel certain, what she had done to him, to his life.''

''You almost sound as though you feel it was right for him to kill her.''

He stared at me, eyes briefly wide in shock. ''Oh, no,'' he said. ''Never that. One does not play God. It is God's province to punish and reward, to give and to take away. It is not Man's.''

I reached for the doorknob, hesitated. ''What did you say to Richard?''

''I scarcely remember. There was little to be said, and I'm afraid I was in too deep a state of personal shock to be very communicative. My son asked my forgiveness. I gave him my blessing. I told him he should look to the Lord for forgiveness." At close range his blue eyes were magnified by the thick lenses. There were tears in their corners. "I only hope he did," he said. "I only hope he did."

EIGHT

I got out of bed while the sky was still dark. I still had the same headache I'd gone to bed with. I went into the bathroom, swallowed a couple of aspirins, then forced myself to put in some time under a hot shower. By the time I was dry and dressed, the headache was mostly gone and the sky was starting to brighten up.

My head was full of fragments of conversation from the night before. I'd returned from Brooklyn with a headache and a thirst, and I'd treated the second more thoroughly than the first. I remember a sketchy conversation with Anita on Long Island—the boys were fine, they were sleeping now, they'd like to come in to New York and see me, maybe stay overnight if it was convenient. I'd said that would be great, but I was working on a case right now. "The cobbler's children always go barefoot," I told her. I don't think she knew what I was talking about.

I got to Armstrong's just as Trina was going off duty. I bought her a couple of stingers and told her a little about the case I was working on. "His mother died when he was six or seven years old," I said. "I hadn't known that."

"Does it make a difference, Matt?"

"I don't know."

After she left I sat by myself and had a few more drinks. I was going to have a hamburger toward the end, but they had already closed the kitchen. I don't know what time I got back to my room. I didn't notice, or didn't remember.

I had breakfast and a lot of coffee next door at the Red Flame. I thought about calling Hanniford at his office. I decided it could wait.

The clerk in the branch post office on Christopher Street informed me that forwarding addresses were only kept active for a year. I suggested that he could check the back files, and he said it wasn't his job and it could be very time-consuming and he was overworked as it was. That would have made him the first overworked postal employee since Benjamin Franklin. I took a hint and palmed him a ten-dollar bill. He seemed surprised, either at the amount or at being given anything at all besides an argument. He went off into a back room and returned a few minutes later with an address for Marcia Maisel on East Eighty-fourth near York Avenue.

The building was a high-rise with underground parking and a lobby that would have served a small airport. There was a little waterfall with pebbles and plastic plants. I couldn't find a Maisel in the directory of tenants. The doorman had never heard of her. I managed to find the super, and he recognized the name. He said she'd gotten married a few months ago and moved out. Her married name was Mrs. Gerald Thal. He had an address for her in Mamaroneck.

I got her number from Westchester Information and dialed it. It was busy the first three times. The fourth time around it rang twice and a woman answered.

I said, "Mrs. Thal?"

"Yes?"

"My name is Matthew Scudder. I'd like to talk to you about Wendy Hanniford."

There was a long silence, and I wondered if I had the right person after all. I'd found a stack of old magazines in a closet of Wendy's apartment with Marcia Maisel's name and the Bethune Street address on them. It was possible that there had been a false connection somewhere along the way—the postal clerk could have pulled the wrong Maisel, the superintendent could have picked the wrong card out of his file.

Then she said, "What do you want from me?"

"I want to ask you a few questions."

"Why me?"

"You lived in the Bethune Street apartment with her."

"That was a long time ago." Long ago, and in another country. And besides, the wench is dead. "I haven't seen Wendy in years. I don't even know if I would recognize her. Would *have* recognized her."

"But you did know her at one time."

"So what? Would you hold on? I have to get a cigarette." I held on. She returned after a moment and said, "I read about it in the newspapers, of course. The boy who did it killed himself, didn't he?"

"Yes."

"Then why drag me into it?"

The fact that she didn't want to be dragged into it was almost reason enough in itself. But I explained the nature of my particular mission, Cale Hanniford's need to know about the recent past of his daughter now that she had no future. When I had finished she told me that she guessed she could answer some questions.

"You moved from Bethune Street to East Eighty-fourth Street a year ago last June."

"How do you know so much about me? Never mind, go on."

"I wondered why you moved."

"I wanted a place of my own."

"I see."

"Plus it was nearer my work. I had a job on the East Side, and it was a hassle getting there from the Village."

"How did you happen to room with Wendy in the first place?"

"She had an apartment that was too big for her, and I needed a place to stay. It seemed like a good idea at the time."

"But it didn't turn out to be a good idea?"

"Well, the location, and also I like my privacy."

She was going to give me whatever answers would get rid of me most efficiently. I wished I were talking to her face-to-face instead of over the telephone. At the same time I hoped I wouldn't have to kill a day driving out to Mamaroneck.

"How did you happen to share the apartment?"

"I just told you, she had a place—"

"Did you answer an ad?"

"Oh, I see what you mean. No, I ran into her on the street, as a matter of fact."

"You had known her previously?"

"Oh, I thought you realized. I knew her at college. I didn't know her well, we were never close, see, but it was a small college and everybody more or less knew everybody, and I ran into her on the street and we got to talking."

"You knew her at college."

"Yeah, I thought you realized. You seem to know so many facts about me, I'm surprised you didn't know that."

"I'd like to come out and talk with you, Mrs. Thal."

"Oh, I don't think so."

"I realize it's an imposition on your time, but—"

"I just don't want to get involved," she said. "Can't you understand that? Jesus Christ, Wendy's dead, right? So what can it help her? Right?"

"Mrs. Thal—"

"I'm hanging up now," she said. And did.

I bought a newspaper, went to a lunch counter and had a cup of coffee. I gave her a full half hour to wonder whether or not I was all that easy to get rid of. Then I dialed her number again.

Something I learned long ago. It is not necessary to know what a person is afraid of. It is enough to know the person is afraid.

She answered in the middle of the second ring. She held the phone to her ear for a moment without saying anything. Then she said, "Hello?"

"This is Scudder."

"Listen, I don't—"

"Shut up a minute, you foolish bitch. I intend

75

to talk to you. I'll either talk to you in front of your husband or I'll talk to you alone.''

Silence.

"Now you just think about it. I can pick up a car and be in Mamaroneck in an hour. An hour after that I'll be back in my car and out of your life. That's the easy way. If you want it the hard way I can oblige you but I don't see that it makes much sense for either of us.''

"Oh, God.''

I let her think about it. The hook was set now, and there was no way she was going to shake it loose.

She said, "Today's impossible. Some friends are coming over for coffee, they'll be here any minute.''

"Tonight?''

"No. Gerry'll be home. Tomorrow?''

"Morning or afternoon?''

"I have a doctor's appointment at ten. I'm free after that.''

"I'll be at your place at noon.''

"No. Wait a minute. I don't want you coming to the house.''

"Pick a place and I'll meet you.''

"Just give me a minute. Christ. I don't even know this area, we just moved here a few months ago. Let me think. There's a restaurant and cocktail lounge on Schuyler Boulevard. It's called the Carioca. I could stop there for lunch after I get out of the doctor's.''

"Noon?''

"All right. I don't know the address.''

"I'll find it. The Carioca on Schuyler Boulevard.''

"Yes. I don't remember your name."

"Scudder. Matthew Scudder."

"How will I recognize you?"

I thought, I'll be the man who looks out of place. I said, "I'll be drinking coffee at the bar."

"All right. I guess we'll find each other."

"I'm sure we will."

My illegal entry the night before had yielded little hard data beyond Marcia Maisel's name. The search of the premises had been complicated by my not knowing precisely what I was searching for. When you toss a place, it helps if you have something specific in mind. It also helps if you don't care whether or not you leave traces of your visit. You can search a few shelves of books far more efficiently, for example, if you feel free to flip through them and then toss them in a heap on the rug. A twenty-minute job stretches out over a couple of hours when you have to put each volume neatly back in place.

There were few enough books in Wendy's apartment, and I hadn't bothered with them, anyway. I wasn't looking for something which had been deliberately concealed. I didn't know what I was looking for, and now, after the fact, I wasn't at all sure what I had found.

I had spent most of my hour wandering through those rooms, sitting on chairs, leaning against walls, trying to rub up against the essence of the two people who had lived here. I looked at the bed Wendy had died on, a double box spring and mattress on a Hollywood frame. They had not yet stripped off the blood-soaked sheets, though there would be little point in doing so; the mattress was deeply soaked with her blood, and the whole bed would have to be scrapped. At one point I stood holding a clot of rusty blood in my hand, and my mind reeled with images of a priest offering Communion. I found the bathroom and gagged without bringing anything up.

While I was there, I pushed the shower curtain aside and examined the tub. There was a ring around it from the last bath taken in it, and some hair matted at the drain, but there was nothing to suggest that anyone had been killed in it. I had not suspected that there would be. Richie Vanderpoel's recapitulation had not been a model of concise linear thought.

The medicine cabinet told me that Wendy had taken birth-control pills. They came in a little card with a dial indicating the days of the week so that you could tell whether you were up-to-date or not. Thursday's pill was gone, so I knew one thing she had done the day she died. She had taken her pill.

Along with the birth-control pills I found enough bottles of organic vitamins to suggest that either or both of the apartment's occupants had been a believer. A small vial with a prescription label indicated that Richie had suffered from hay fever. There was quite a bit in the way of cosmetics, two different brands of deodorant, a small electric razor for shaving legs and underarms, a large electric razor for shaving faces. I found some other prescription drugs—Seconal and Darvon (his), Dexedrine spansules labeled *For Weight Control* (hers), and an unlabeled bottle containing what looked like Librium. I was surprised the drugs were still around. Cops are apt to pocket them, and men who would not take loose cash from the dead have trouble resisting the little pills that pick you up or settle you down.

I took the Seconal and the Dex along with me.

A closet and a dresser in the bedroom filled with her clothes. Not a large wardrobe, but several dresses had labels from Bloomingdale's and Lord & Taylor. His clothes were in the living room. One of the closets there was his, and he kept shirts and socks and underwear in the drawers of a Spanish-style kneehole desk.

The living-room couch was a convertible. I opened it up and found it made up with sheets and blankets. The sheets had been slept on since their last laundering. I closed the couch and sat on it.

A well-equipped kitchen, copper-bottomed frying pans, a set of burnt-orange enameled cast-iron pots and pans, a teak rack with thirty-two jars of herbs and spices. The refrigerator held a couple of TV dinners in the freezer compartment, but the rest of it was abundantly stocked with real food. So were the cupboards. The kitchen was a large one by Manhattan standards, and there was a round oak table in it. There were two captain's chairs at the table. I sat at one of them and pictured cozy domestic scenes, one of them whipping up a gourmet meal, the two of them sitting at this table and eating it.

I had left the apartment without finding the helpful things one hopes to find. No address books, no checkbooks, no bank statements. No revealing stacks of canceled checks. Whatever their financial arrangements, they had evidently conducted them on a cash basis.

Now, a day later, I thought of my impressions of that apartment and tried to match them up with

Martin Vanderpoel's portrait of Wendy as evil incarnate. If she had trapped him with sex, why did he sleep on a folding bed in the living room? And why did the whole apartment have such an air of placid domesticity to it, a comfortable domesticity that all the blood in the bedroom could not entirely drown?

NINE

When I got back to my hotel there was a phone message at the desk. Cale Hanniford had called at a quarter after eleven. I was to call him. He had left a number, and it was one he had already given me. His office number.

I called him from my room. He was at lunch. His secretary said he would call me back. I said no, I'd try him again in an hour or so.

The call reminded me of J.J. Cottrell, Inc., Wendy's employment reference on her lease application. I found the number in my notebook and tried it again on the chance I'd misdialed it first time around. I got the same recording. I checked the telephone directory for J.J. Cottrell and didn't come up with anything. I tried Information, and they didn't have anything, either.

I thought for a few minutes, then dialed a special number. When a woman picked up, I said, "Patrolman Lewis Pankow, Sixth Precinct. I have a listing that's temporarily out of service, and I have to know in what name it's listed."

She asked the number. I gave it to her. She asked me to please hold the line. I sat there with the phone against my ear for almost ten minutes before she came back on the line.

"That's not a temporary disconnect," she said. "That's a permanent disconnect."

"Can you tell me who the number was assigned to last?"

"I'm afraid I can't, officer."

"Don't you keep that information on file?"

"We must have it somewhere, but I don't have access to it. I have recent disconnects, but that was disconnected over a year ago, so I wouldn't have it. I'm surprised it hasn't been reassigned by now."

"So all you know is that it's been out of service for more than a year."

That was all she knew. I thanked her and rang off. I poured myself a drink, and by the time it was gone I decided that Hanniford ought to be back in his office. I was right.

He told me he had managed to find the post-cards. The first one, postmarked New York, had been mailed on June 4. The second had been mailed in Miami on September 16.

"Does that tell you anything, Scudder?"

It told me she had been in New York in early June if not before then. It told me she had taken the Miami trip prior to signing the lease on her apartment. Beyond that, it didn't tell me a tremendous amount.

"Another piece of the puzzle," I said. "Do you have the cards with you now?"

"Yes, they're right in front of me."

"Could you read me the messages?"

"They don't say very much." I waited, and he said, "Well, there's no reason not to read them. This is the first card. 'Dear Mom and Dad. Hope you haven't been worrying about me. Everything is fine. Am in New York and like the big city very much. School got to be too much of a hassle. Will explain everything when I see you.'" His voice cracked a little on that line, but he coughed and went on. "'Please don't worry. Love, Wendy.'"

"And the other card?"

"Hardly anything on it. 'Dear Mom and Dad. Not bad, huh? I always thought Florida was strictly for wintertime, but it's great this time of year. See you soon. Love, Wendy.'"

He asked me how things were going. I didn't really know how to answer the question. I said I had been very busy and was putting a lot of bits and pieces together but that I didn't know when I would have something to show him. "Wendy was sharing her apartment with another girl for several months before Vanderpoel came on the scene."

"Was the other girl a prostitute?"

"I don't know. I rather doubt it, but I'm not sure. I'm seeing her tomorrow. Evidently she was someone Wendy knew at college. Did she ever mention a friend named Marcia Maisel?"

"Maisel? I don't think so."

"Do you know the names of any of her frineds from college?"

"I don't believe I do. Let me think. I seem to recall that she would refer to them by first names, and they didn't stick in my mind."

"It's probably unimportant. Does the name Cottrell mean anything to you?"

"Cottrell?" I spelled it, and he said it aloud

again. "No, it doesn't mean anything to me. Should it?"

"Wendy used a firm by that name as a job reference when she signed her apartment lease. The firm doesn't seem to exist."

"Why did you think I would have heard of it?"

"Just a shot in the dark. I've been taking a lot of them lately, Mr. Hanniford. Was Wendy a good cook?"

"Wendy? Not as far as I know. Of course she may have developed an interest in cooking at college. I wouldn't know about that. When she was living at home, I don't think she ever made anything more ambitious than a peanut-butter-and-jelly sandwich. Why?"

"No reason."

His other phone rang, and he asked if there was anything else. I started to say that there wasn't and then thought of what I should have thought of at the beginning. "The postcards," I said.

"What about them?"

"What's on the other side?"

"The other side?"

"They're picture postcards, aren't they? Turn them over. I want to know what's on the other side."

"I'll see. Grant's Tomb. Is that an important piece of the puzzle, Scudder?"

I ignored the sarcasm. "That's New York," I said. "I'm more interested in the Miami one."

"It's a hotel."

"What hotel?"

"Oh, for Christ's sake. I didn't even think of it that way. It could mean something, couldn't it?"

"What hotel, Mr. Hanniford?"

"The Eden Roc. Does that give you an important lead?"

It didn't.

I got the manager at the Eden Roc and told him I was a New York City police officer investigating a fraud case. I had him dig out his registration cards for the month of September 1970. I was on the phone for half an hour while he located the cards and went through them, looking for a registration in the name of either Hanniford or Cottrell. He came up empty.

I wasn't too surprised. Cottrell didn't have to be the man who took her to Miami. Even if he was, that didn't mean he would necessarily sign his real name on a registration card. It would have made life simpler if he had, but nothing about Wendy Hanniford's life and death had been simple so far, and I couldn't expect a sudden rush of simplicity now.

I poured another drink and decided to let the rest of the day spin itself out. I was trying to do too much, trying to sift all the sand in the desert. Pointless, because I was looking for answers to questions my client hadn't even asked. It didn't much matter who Richie Vanderpoel was, or why he had drawn red lines on Wendy. All Hanniford wanted was a hint of the life that late she led. Mrs. Gerald Thal, the former Miss Marcia Maisel, would provide as much tomorrow.

So until then I could take it easy. Look at the paper, drink my drink, wander over to Armstrong's when the walls of my room moved too close to one another.

Except that I couldn't. I made the drink last

almost half an hour, then rinsed out the glass and put my coat on and caught the A train downtown.

When you hit a gay bar in the middle of a weekday afternoon you wonder why they don't call it something else. In the evenings, with a good crowd drinking and cruising, there is a very real gaiety in the air. It may seem forced, and you may sense an undercurrent of insufficiently quiet desperation, but gay then is about as good a word as any. But not around three or four on a Thursday afternoon, when the place is down to a handful of serious drinkers with no place else to go and a bartender whose face says he knows how bad things are and that he's stopped waiting for them to get better.

I made the rounds. A basement club on Bank Street where a man with long white hair and a waxed moustache played the bowling machine all by himself while his beer went flat. A big room on West Tenth, its ambience pitched for the old college athlete crowd, sawdust on the floor and Greek-letter pennants on the exposed brick walls. In all, half a dozen gay bars within a four-block radius of 194 Bethune Street.

I got stared at a lot. Was I a cop? Or a potential sexual partner? Or both?

I had the newspaper photo of Richie, and I showed it around a lot to whoever was willing to look at it. Almost everyone recognized the photo because they had seen it in the paper. The murder was recent, and it had happened right in the neighborhood, and heterosexuals have no monopoly on morbid curiosity. So most of them recognized the picture, and quite a few had seen him in the neighborhood, or said they had, but nobody recalled seeing him around the bars.

"Of course I don't come here all that often," I heard more than once. "Just drop in now and then for a beer when the throat gets scratchy."

In a place called Sinthia's the bartender recognized me and did an elaborate double take. "Do my eyes deceive me? Or is it really the one and only Matthew Scudder?"

"Hello, Ken."

"Now don't tell me you've finally converted, Matt. It was enough of a shock when I heard you left the pigpen. If Matthew Scudder's come around to the belief that Gay is Good, why, I'd be properly devastated."

He still looked twenty-eight, and he must have been almost twice that. The blond hair was his own, even if the color came out of a bottle. When you got up close you could see the face-lift lines, but from a couple of yards away he didn't look a day older than when I'd booked him fifteen years ago for contributing to the delinquency of a minor. I hadn't taken much pride in the collar; the minor had been seventeen, and had already been more delinquent than Ken had ever hoped to be, but the minor had a father and the father filed a complaint and I had had to pick Kenny up. He got himself a decent lawyer, and the charges were dropped.

"You're looking good," I told him.

"Booze and tobacco and lots of sex. It keeps a lad young."

"Ever see this young lad?" I dropped the news photo on top of the bar. He looked at it, then gave it back.

"Interesting."

"You recognize him?"

"It's the young chap who was so nasty last week, isn't it? Ghastly story."

"Yes."

"Where do you come in?"

"It's hard to say. Ever see him in here, Kenny?"

He planted his elbows on the bar and made a V of his hands, then tucked his chin between them. "The reason I said it was interesting," he said, "is that I thought I recognized that picture when the *Post* ran it. I have an extraordinary memory for faces. Among other anatomical areas."

"You've seen him before."

"I *thought* so, and now I find myself certain of it. Why don't you buy us each a drink while I comb my memory?"

I put a bill on the bar. He poured bourbon for me and mixed something orange for himself. He said, "I'm not stalling, Matthew. I am trying to recall what went with the face. I know I haven't seen it in a long time."

"How long?"

"At least a year." He sipped at his drink, straightened up, clasped his hands behind his neck, closed his eyes. "A year at the very least. I remember him now. Very attractive. And *very* young. I asked him for ID the first time he came in, and he didn't seem surprised, as if he always got asked for proof of age."

"He was only nineteen then."

"Well, he could have passed for a ripe sixteen. There was a period of a couple of weeks when he was in here almost every night. Then I never saw him again."

"I gather he was gay."

"Well, he wouldn't have come here to pick up girls, would he?"

"He could have been window shopping."

"Too true. We do get our fair share of those, don't we? Not Richie, though. He wasn't much of a drinker, you know. He'd order a vodka Collins and make it last until all the ice had melted."

"Not a very profitable customer."

"Oh, when they're young and gorgeous you don't care whether they spend much. They're window dressing, you know. They bring others in. From window shopping to window dressing, and no, our lad was not just looking, thank you. I don't think there was a night he came here that he didn't let someone take him home."

He moved to the other end of the bar to replenish someone's drink. When he returned I asked him if he had ever taken Vanderpoel home himself.

"Matthew, honey, if I had, I wouldn't have had that much trouble remembering him, would I now?"

"You might."

"*Bitch!* No, I was going through a very monogamous period at the time. Don't raise your brows so skeptically, luv. It doesn't become you. I suppose I might have been tempted, but cute as he was, he was not my type."

"I would have thought he'd be just your type."

"Oh, you don't know me as well as you think you do, do you, Matthew? I like a bit of chicken now and then, I'll admit it. God knows it's not the world's best-kept secret in the first place. But it's not just youth that does it for me, you know. It's corrupt youth."

"Oh?"

"That luscious air of immature decadence. Young fruit rotting on the vines."

"You have a lovely way of putting things."

"Don't I? But Richard was not like that at all. He had this untouchable innocence. You could be his eighth trick of the night, and you would still feel that you were seducing a virgin. And that, dear boy, is not my scene at all, as the children say."

He made himself a fresh drink and collected for it out of my change. I still had enough bourbon left. I said, "You said something about the eighth trick of the night. Was he selling himself?"

"No way. He didn't get the chance to pay for his own drinks, but if he had one drink a night, it was a lot. He wasn't hustling a buck."

"Was he running the numbers?"

"No, one partner a night was all he seemed to want. As far as I could tell."

"And then he stopped coming in here. I wonder why."

"Maybe he got allergic to the decor."

"Was there anyone in particular he tended to go home with?"

Ken shook his head. "Never the same friend twice. I would guess that he came around over a period of three weeks, and maybe he paid us fifteen or eighteen visits in all, and I never saw him repeat. That's not terribly unusual, you know. A lot of people are hung up on variety. Especially the young ones."

"He started living with Wendy Hanniford around the time he stopped coming here."

"I gathered he was living with her. I wouldn't

know about the time element.''

''Why would he live with a woman, Ken?''

''I didn't really know him, Matt. And I'm not a psychiatrist. I *had* a psychiatrist, but that wasn't one of the topics we got around to discussing.''

''Why would any homosexual live with a woman?''

''God knows.''

''Seriously, Kenny.''

He drummed the bar with his fingers. ''Seriously? All right. He could be bisexual, you know. It's not exactly unheard of, especially in this day and age. Everybody's doing it, I understand. Straight types are trying the gay scene on for size. Gay types are making tentative experiments with heterosexuality.'' He yawned elaborately. ''I'm afraid I'm a hopelessly reactionary old thing myself. One sex is complicated enough for me. Two would be disastrous.''

''Any other ideas?''

''Not really. If I'd *known* him, Matt. But he was just another pretty face to me.''

''Who knew him?''

''Does anyone know anyone? I suppose whoever took him to bed came closest to knowing him.''

''Who took him to bed?''

''I'm not a scorekeeper, darling. And we've had quite the turnover here these past few months. Most of the old crowd has gone off in search of greener pastures. We're getting a lot of smarmy little leather boys lately.'' He frowned at the thought, then remembered that frowning gives you lines and willed his face to return to its normal expression. ''I don't much adore the crew we've been attracting lately. Motorcycle boys, S-and-M types. I don't really want anyone killed in my bar, you know. Most especially my estimable self."

"Why not do something about it?"

"To be horribly candid, they scare me."

I finished my drink. "There's an easy way for you to handle it."

"Do tell."

"Go over to the Sixth Precinct and talk to Lieutenant Edward Koehler. Tell him your problem and ask him to raid you a few times."

"You've got to be kidding."

"Think about it. Slip Koehler a couple of bucks. Fifty should do it. He'll arrange to raid you a few times and give your leather crowd a hard time. There won't be any charges against you, so it won't screw you up with the SLA. Your liquor license won't be in jeopardy. The motorcycle boys are like everybody else. They can't afford hassles. They'll find some other house to haunt. Of course your business will fall off for a couple of weeks."

"It's off, anyway. The little cunts are all beer drinkers, and they don't leave tips."

"So you won't be losing much. Then in a month or so you'll start getting the kind of clientele you want."

"What a devious mind you have, Matthew. I think it might work, at that."

"It should. And don't give me too much credit. It's done all the time."

"You say fifty dollars should do it?"

"It ought to. It would have when I was on the force, but everything's been going up lately, even bribery. If Koehler wants more, he'll let you know about it."

"I don't doubt it. Well, it's not as if I never gave money to New York's Finest. They come around every Friday to collect, and you wouldn't believe what Christmas cost me."

"Yes, I would."

"But I never gave them money in the hope of anything beyond being allowed to remain in business. I didn't realize you could ask favors in return."

"It's a free-enterprise system."

"So it seems. I just might try it, and I'll buy you a drink on the strength of it."

He poured a generous shot into my glass. I picked it up and eyed him over the top of it. "There's something else you could do for me," I said.

"Oh?"

"Ask around a little about Richie Vanderpoel. I know you don't want to give me any names. That's reasonable. But see if you can find out what he was like. I'd appreciate it."

"Don't expect much."

"I won't."

He ran his fingers through his beautiful blond hair. "Do you really *care* what he was like, Matt?"

"Yes," I said. "Evidently I do."

Maybe it was a reaction to too many visits to bars that were gay in name alone. I'm not sure, but on my way to the subway I stopped at an outdoor phone booth and looked up a number in my notebook. I dropped in a dime and dialed it, and when she answered I said, "Elaine? Matt Scudder."

"Oh, hi, Matt. How's it going?"

"Not too bad. I was wondering if you felt like company."

"I'd love to see you. Give me a half hour? I was just getting into the shower."

"Sure."

I had coffee and a roll and read the *Post*. The new mayor was having trouble appointing a deputy mayor. His investigative board kept discovering that his prospective appointees were corrupt in any of several uninteresting ways. There was an obvious answer, and he would probably hit on it sooner or later. He was going to have to get rid of the investigative board.

Some more citizens had killed each other since yesterday's edition went to press. Two off-duty patrolmen had had a few drinks in a bar in Woodside and shot each other with their service revolvers. One was dead, the other in critical condition. A man and woman who had served ninety days each for child abuse had sued successfully to regain custody of the child from the foster parents who had had the kid for three and a half years. The nude torso of an adolescent boy had been discovered on a tenement roof on East Fifth Street. Someone had carved an X into the chest, presumably the same person who had removed the arms and legs and head.

I left the newspaper on the table and got a cab.

She lived in a good building on Fifty-first between First and Second. The doorman confirmed that I was expected and nodded me toward the elevator. She was waiting at the door for me, wearing royal-blue hip-huggers and a lime-green blouse. She had gold hoop earrings in her ears and she smelled of a rich, musky perfume.

I draped my coat over an Eames chair while she closed the door and fastened the bolt. She came into my arms for an openmouthed kiss and rubbed her little body against me. "Mmmm," she said. "That's nice."

"You're looking good, Elaine."

"Let me look at you. You don't look so bad yourself, in a rugged, rough-hewn sort of a way. How've you been?"

"Pretty good."

"Keeping busy?"

"Uh-huh."

There was chamber music stacked on her stereo. The last record was just ending, and I sat on the couch and watched as she walked to the turntable and inverted the stack of records. I wondered whether the hip wiggle was for my benefit or if it came naturally to her. I had always wondered that.

I liked the room. White wall-to-wall shag carpet, stark modern furniture more comfortable than it looked, a lot of primary colors and chrome. A couple of abstract oils on the walls. I couldn't have lived in a room like that, but I enjoyed spending occasional time in it.

"Drink?"

"Not just now."

She sat on the couch next to me and talked about books she had read and movies she had seen. She was very good at small talk. I suppose she had to be.

We kissed a few times, and I touched her breasts and put a hand on her round bottom. She made a purring sound.

"Want to come to bed, Matt?"

"Sure."

The bedroom was small, with a more subdued color scheme. She turned on a small stained-glass lamp and killed the overhead light. We got undressed and lay down on the queen-size bed.

She was warm and young and eager, with soft, perfumed skin and a tautly muscled body. Her hands and mouth were clever. But it was not working, and after a few minutes I moved away from her and patted her gently on the shoulder.

"Relax, honey."

"No, it's not going to work," I said.

"Something I should be doing?"

I shook my head.

"Too much to drink?"

It wasn't that. I was far too completely locked into my own head. "Maybe," I said.

"It happens."

"Or maybe it's the wrong time of the month for me."

She laughed. "Right, you got your period."

"Must be."

We put our clothes on. I got three tens from my wallet and put them on the dresser. As usual, she pretended not to notice.

"Want that drink now?"

"Uh-huh, I guess. Bourbon, if you have it."

She didn't. She had Scotch, and I settled for that. She poured herself a glass of milk, and we sat on the couch together and listened to the music without saying anything for a while. I felt as relaxed as if we had made love.

"Working these days, Matt?"

"Uh-huh."

"Well, everybody has to work."

"Uh-huh."

She shook a cigarette out of her pack, and I lit it for her. "You got things on your mind," she said. "That's what's the matter."

"You're probably right."

"I know I'm right. Want to talk about anything?"

"Not really."

"Okay."

The telephone rang, and she answered it in the bedroom. When she came back I asked her if she had ever lived with a man.

"You mean like a pimp? Never have and never will."

"I meant like a boyfriend."

"Never. It's a funny thing about boyfriends in this business. They always turn out to be pimps."

"Really?"

"Uh-huh. I've known so many girls. 'Oh, he's not a pimp, he's my boyfriend.' But it always turns out that he's between jobs, and that he makes a life's work out of being between jobs, and she pays for everything. But he's not a pimp, just a boyfriend. They're very good at kidding themselves, those girls. I'm lousy at kidding myself. So I don't even try."

"Good for you."

"I can't afford boyfriends. Busy saving for my old age."

"Real estate, right?"

"Uh-huh. Apartment houses in Queens. You can keep the stock market. I want something I can reach out and touch."

"You're a landlady. That's funny."

"Oh, I never see tenants or anything. There's a company manages it for me."

I wondered if it was Bowdoin Management but didn't bother asking. She asked if I wanted to try the bedroom again. I said I didn't.

"Not to rush you, but I'm expecting a friend in about forty minutes."

"Sure."

"Have another drink if you want."

"No, it's time I was on my way." She walked me to the door and held my coat for me. I kissed her goodbye.

"Don't be so long between visits next time."

"Take care, Elaine."

"Oh, I will."

TEN

Friday morning came clear and crisp. I picked up an Olin rental car on Broadway and took the East Side Drive out of town. The car was a Chevrolet Malibu, a skittish little thing that had to be pampered on curves. I suppose it was economical to run.

I caught the New England Expressway up through Pelham and Larchmont and into Mamaroneck. At an Exxon station the kid who topped up the tank didn't know where Schuyler Boulevard was. He went inside and asked the boss, who came out and gave me directions. The boss also knew the Carioca, and I had the Malibu parked in the restaurant's lot at twenty-five minutes of twelve. I went into the cocktail lounge and sat on a vinyl stool at the front end of a black Formica bar. I ordered a cup of black coffee with a shot of bourbon in it. The coffee was bitter, left over from the night before.

The cup was still half full when I looked over and saw her standing hesitantly in the archway between the dining room and the cocktail lounge.

If I hadn't known she was Wendy Hanniford's age, I would have guessed high by three or four years. Dark, shoulder-length hair framed an oval face. She wore dark plaid slacks and a pearl-gray sweater beneath which her large breasts were aggressively prominent. She had a large brown leather handbag over her shoulder and a cigarette in her right hand. She did not look happy to see me.

I let her come to me, and after a moment's hesitation she did. I turned slowly to her.

"Mr. Scudder?"

"Mrs. Thal? Should we take a table?"

"I suppose so."

The dining room was uncrowded, and the head waitress showed us to a table in back and out of the way. It was an overdecorated room, a room that tried too hard, done in someone's idea of a flamenco motif. The color scheme involved a lot of red and black and ice blue. I had left my bitter coffee at the bar and now ordered bourbon with water back. I asked Marcia Thal if she wanted a drink.

"No, thank you. Wait a minute. Yes, I think I will have something. Why shouldn't I?"

"No reason that I know of."

She looked past me at the waitress and ordered a whiskey sour on the rocks. Her eyes met mine, glanced away, came back again.

"I can't say I'm happy to be here," she said.

"Neither am I."

"It was your idea. And you had me over a barrel, didn't you? You must get a kick out of making people do what you want them to do."

"I used to pull wings off flies."

"I wouldn't be surprised." She tried to glare,

and then she lost the handle of it and grinned in spite of herself. "Oh, shit," she said.

"You're not going to be dragged into anything, Mrs. Thal."

"I hope not."

"You won't be. I'm interested in learning something about Wendy Hanniford's life. I'm not interested in turning your life upside down."

Our drinks arrived. She picked hers up and studied it as if she had never seen anything quite like it before. It seemed an ordinary enough whiskey sour. She took a sip, set it down, fished out the maraschino cherry and ate it. I swallowed a little bourbon and waited for her.

"You can order something to eat if you want. I'm not hungry."

"Neither am I."

"I don't know where to start. I really don't."

I wasn't sure myself. I said, "Wendy doesn't seem to have had a job. Was she working when you first moved in with her?"

"No. But I didn't know that."

"She told you she had a job?"

She nodded. "But she was always very vague about it. I didn't pay too much attention, to tell you the truth. I was mainly interested in Wendy to the extent that she had an apartment I could share for a hundred dollars a month."

"That's all she charged you?"

"Yes. At the time she told me the apartment was two hundred a month and we were splitting it down the middle. I never saw the lease or anything, and I sort of assumed that I was paying a little more than half. That was all right with me. It was her furniture and everything, and it was such a bargain for me. Before that I was at the Evangeline House. Do you know what that is?''

"On West Thirteenth?''

"That's right. Somebody recommended it to me, it's a residence for proper young ladies on their own in the big city." She made a face. "They had curfews and things like that. It was really pretty ridiculous, and I was sharing a small room with a girl, she was some kind of a Southern Baptist and she was praying all the time, and you couldn't have male visitors, and it was all pretty lame. And it cost me almost as much as it cost to share the apartment with Wendy. So if she was making a little money on me, that was fine. It wasn't until quite a bit later that I found out the apartment was renting for a lot more than two hundred a month."

"And she wasn't working."

"No."

"Did you wonder where her money came from?"

"Not for a while. I gradually managed to realize that she never seemed to have to go to the office, and when I said something, she admitted she was between jobs at the moment. She said she had enough money so that she didn't care if she didn't find anything for a month or two. What I didn't realize was that she wasn't even looking for work. I would come home from my own job, and she would say something about employment agencies and job interviews, and I would have no way of knowing that she hadn't even been looking."

"Was she a prositute at the time?"

"I don't know if you would call it that."

"How do you mean?"

"She was taking money from men. I guess she had been doing that for as long as she was in the

"I thought she was a tramp," she said. "I'm not a moralist, Mr. Scudder. During that time I was probably going overboard in the opposite direction. Not in terms of how I behaved, but how I felt about things. All those uptight virgins at Evangeline House, and the result was that I had sort of mixed feelings about Wendy."

"How?"

"I thought what she was doing was probably a bad idea. That it would be bad for her emotionally. You know, ego damage, that kind of thing. Because down underneath she was always so innocent."

"Innocent?"

She gnawed a fingernail. "I don't know how to explain this. There was this little girl quality to her. I had the feeling that whatever kind of sex life she led she would still be a little girl underneath it all." She thought for a moment, then shrugged. "Anyway, I thought her behavior was basically self-destructive. I thought she was going to get hurt."

"You don't mean physically injured."

"No, I mean emotionally. And at the same time I have to say I envied her."

"Because she was free?"

"Yes. She didn't seem to have any hang-ups. She was completely free of guilt as far as I could see. She did whatever she wanted to do. I envied that because I believed in that kind of freedom, or thought I did, and yet my own life didn't reflect it." She grinned suddenly. "I also envied her life because it was so much more exciting than mine. I had some dates but nothing very interesting, and the boys I went out with were around my own age and didn't have much money. Wendy was going out for dinners at places like Barbetta's and the Forum, and I was seeing the inside of a lot of Orange Julius's. So I couldn't help envying her a little."

She excused herself and went to the ladies room. While she was gone I asked the waitress if there was any fresh coffee. She said there was, and I asked her to bring a couple of cups. I sat there waiting for Marcia Thal and wondering why Wendy had wanted a roommate in the first place, especially one who was ignorant of how she earned her keep. The hundred dollars a month seemed insufficient motive, and the inconvenience of functioning as a prostitute under the conditions Marcia had described would have greatly outweighed the small source of income Marcia represented.

She returned to the table just as the waitress was bringing the coffee. "Thanks," she said. "I was just starting to feel those drinks. I can use this."

"So can I. I've got a long drive back."

She took a cigarette. I picked up a pack of matches and lit it for her. I asked how she had found out that Wendy was taking money for her favors.

"She told me."

"Why?"

"Hell," she said. She blew out smoke in a long, thin column. "She just told me, okay? Let's leave it at that."

"It's a lot easier if you just tell me everything, Marcia."

"What makes you think there's anything more to tell?"

"What did she do, pass on one of her dates to you?"

Her eyes flared. She closed them briefly, drew on her cigarette. "It was almost like that," she said. "Not quite, but that's pretty close. She told me a friend of hers had a business associate in from out of town and asked if I'd like to date the guy, to double with her and her friend. I said I didn't think so, and she talked about how we would see a good show and have a good dinner and everything. And then she said, 'Be sensible, Marcia. You'll have a good time, and you'll make a few dollars out of it.' "

"How did you react?"

"Well, I wasn't shocked. So I must have suspected all along that she was getting money. I asked her what she meant, which was a pretty stupid question at that point, and she said that the men she dated all had plenty of money, and they realized it was tough for a young woman to earn a decent living, and at the end of the evening they would generally give you something. I said something about wasn't that prostitution, and she said she never asked men for money, nothing like that, but they always gave her something. I wanted to ask how much but I didn't and then she told me anyway. She said they always gave at least twenty dollars and sometimes a man would give her as much as a hundred. The man she was going to be seeing always gave her fifty dollars, she said, so if I went along it would mean that his friend would be almost certain to give me fifty dollars, and she asked if I didn't think that was a good return on an evening that involved nothing but eating a great dinner and seeing a good show and then spending a half hour or so in bed with a nice, dignified gentleman. That was her phrase. 'A nice, dignified gentleman.' "

"How did the date go?"

"What makes you so sure I went?"

"You did, didn't you?"

"I was earning eighty dollars a week. Nobody was taking me to great dinners or Broadway shows. And I hadn't even met anyone I wanted to sleep with."

"Did you enjoy the evening?"

"No. All I could think about was that I was going to have to sleep with this man. And he was *old*."

"How old?"

"I don't know. Fifty-five, sixty. I'm never good at guessing how old people are. He was too old for me, that's all I knew."

"But you went along with it."

"Yes. I had agreed to go, and I didn't want to spoil the party. Dinner was good, and my date was charming enough. I didn't pay much attention to the show. I couldn't. I was too anxious about the rest of the evening." She paused, focused her eyes over my shoulder. "Yes, I slept with him. And yes, he gave me fifty dollars. And yes, I took it."

I drank some coffee.

"Aren't you going to ask me why I took the money?"

"Should I?"

"I wanted the damned money. And I wanted to know how it felt. Being a whore."

"Did you feel that you were a whore?"

"Well, that's what I was, isn't it? I let a man fuck me, and I took money for it."

I didn't say anything. After a few moments she said, "Oh, the hell with it. I took a few more dates. Maybe one a week on the average. I don't know why. It wasn't the money. Not exactly. It was, I don't know. Call it an experiment. I wanted to know how I felt about it. I wanted to . . . learn certain things about myself.''

"What did you learn?"

"That I'm a little squarer than I thought. That I didn't care for the things I kept finding hiding in corners of my mind. That I wanted, oh, a cleaner life. That I wanted to fall in love with somebody. Get married, make babies, that whole trip. It turned out to be what I wanted. When I realized that, I knew I had to move out on my own. I couldn't go on rooming with Wendy.''

"How did she react?"

"She was very upset.'' Her eyes widened at the recollection. ''I hadn't expected that. We weren't terribly close. At least I never thought we were terribly close. I never showed her the inside of my head, and she never showed me what was going on inside hers. We were together a lot, especially once I started taking dates, and we talked a great deal, but it was always about superficial things. I didn't think my presence was especially important to her. I told her I had to move out, and I told her why, and she was really shook. She actually begged me to stay.''

"That's interesting.''

"She told me she'd pay a larger share of the rent. That was when I found out she'd actually been paying twice as much as I was all along, I think she would have let me stay there rent-free if I wanted. And of course she insisted I didn't have to take any dates, that she wouldn't want me to do it if it was putting me uptight. She even suggested that she would limit her activities to times when I was at work—actually a lot of her dates were during the afternoon, businessmen who couldn't get away from their wives during the evening, which was one reason why it took me as long as it did to realize how she was making her living. She said evening dates would have to take her to a hotel or something, that the place would be just for us when I was around. But that wasn't it, I had to get away from the life entirely. Because it was too much of a temptation for me, see. I was making eighty dollars a week and working hard for it, and there was an enormous temptation to quit work, which is something I never did, but I recognized the temptation for what it was. And it scared me.''

"So you moved out."

"Yes. Wendy cried when I packed my stuff and left. She kept saying she didn't know what she would do without me. I told her she could get another roommate without any trouble, someone who would fit in with her life better. She said she didn't want anyone who fit in too well because she was more than one kind of person. I didn't know what she meant at the time.''

"Do you know now?"

"I think so. I think she wanted someone who was a little straighter than she was, someone who was not a part of the sexual scene she was involved in. I think now that she was a little disappointed when I took that first double date with her. She did her best to talk me into it, but she was disappointed that she was successful. Do you know what I mean?''

"I think so. It fits in with some other things." There was something she had said earlier that had been bothering me, and I poked around in my memory, looking for it. "You said you weren't surprised that she was seeing older men."

"No, that didn't surprise me."

"Why not?"

"Well, because of what happened at school."

"What happened at school?"

She frowned. She didn't say anything, and I repeated the question.

"I don't want to get anybody in trouble."

"She was involved with someone at school? An older man?"

"You have to remember I didn't know her very well. I knew who she was to say hello to, and maybe I was in a class or two with her at one time or another, but I barely knew her."

"Was it tied in with her leaving school just a few months shy of graduation?"

"I don't really know that much about it."

I said, "Marcia, look at me. Anything you tell me about what happened at college will be something I would otherwise find out, anyway. You'll just save me a great deal of time and travel. I'd rather not have to make a trip out to Indiana to ask a lot of people some embarrassing questions. I—"

"Oh, don't do that!"

"I'd rather not. But it's up to you."

She told it in bits and pieces, largely because she didn't know too much of it. There had been a scandal shortly before Wendy's departure from campus. It seemed that she had been having an affair with a professor of art history, a middle-aged man with children Wendy's age or older. The man had wanted to leave his wife and marry Wendy, the wife had swallowed a handful of sleeping pills, was rushed to the hospital, had her stomach pumped, and survived. In the course of the ensuing debacle, Wendy packed a suitcase and disappeared.

And according to campus gossip this was not the first time she had been involved with an older man. Her name had been linked with several professors, all of them considerably older than she was.

"I'm sure a lot of it was just talk," Marcia Thal told me. "I don't think she could have had affairs with that many men without more people knowing about it, but when the whole thing blew up, people were really talking about her. I guess some of it must have been true."

"Then you knew when you first roomed with her that she was unconventional."

"I told you. I didn't care about her morals. I didn't see anything wrong with sleeping with a lot of men. Not if that was what she wanted to do." She considered this for a moment. "I guess I've changed since then."

"This professor, the art historian. What was his name?"

"I'm not going to tell you his name. It's not important. Maybe you can find out yourself. I'm sure you can, but *I'm* not going to tell you."

"Was it Cottrell?"

"No. Why?"

"Did she know anyone named Cottrell? In New York?"

"I don't think so. The name doesn't ring a bell or anything."

"Was there anyone she was seeing regularly? More than the others?"

"Not really. Of course she could have had someone who came over a lot during the afternoons and I wouldn't have known it.''

"How much money do you suppose she was making?''

"I don't know. That wasn't really something we talked about. I suppose her average price was thirty dollars. On the average. No more than that. A lot of men gave twenty. She talked about men who would give her a hundred, but I think they were pretty rare.''

"How many tricks a week do you think she turned?''

"I honestly don't know. Maybe she had someone over three nights a week, maybe four nights a week. But she was also seeing people in the daytime. She wasn't trying to make a fortune, just enough to live the way she wanted to live. A lot of the time she would turn down dates. She never saw more than one person a night. It wasn't always a full date with dinner and everything. Sometimes a man would just come over, and she would go straight to bed with him. But she turned down a lot of dates, and if she went with a man and she didn't like him she wouldn't see him again. Also, when she was seeing someone she had never met before, if she didn't like him she wouldn't go to bed with him, and then of course he wouldn't give her any money. There would be men who would get her number from other men, see, and she would go out with them, but if they weren't her type or something, well, she'd say she had a headache and go home. She wasn't trying to make a million dollars.''

"So she must have earned a couple hundred dollars a week.''

"That sounds about right. It was a fortune compared to what I was earning, but in the long run it wasn't a tremendous amount of money. I don't think she did it for the money, if you know what I mean."

"I'm not sure I do."

"I think she was, you know, a happy hooker?" She flushed as she said the phrase. "I think she enjoyed what she was doing. I really do. The life and the men and everything, I think she got a kick out of it."

I had obtained more from Marcia Thal than I'd expected. Maybe it was as much as I needed.

You have to know when to stop. You can never find out everything, but you can almost always find out more than you already know, and there is a point at which the additional data you discover is irrelevant and time you spend on it wasted.

I could fly out to Indiana. I would learn more, certainly. But when I was done I didn't think I would necessarily know more than I did now. I could fill in names and dates. I could talk to people who had memories of their own of Wendy Hanniford. But what would I get for my client?

I signaled for the check. While the waitress was adding things up, I thought of Cale Hanniford and asked Marcia Thal if Wendy had spoken often of her parents.

"Sometimes she talked about her father."

"What did she say about him?"

"Oh, wondering what he was like."

"She felt she didn't know him?"

"Well, of course not. I mean, I gather he died before she was born, or just about. How could she have known him?"

"I meant her stepfather."

"Oh. No, she never talked about him that I

remember, except to say vaguely that she ought to write them and let them know everything was all right. She said that several times, so I got the impression it was something she kept not getting around to."

I nodded. "What did she say about her father?"

"I don't remember, except I guess she idolized him a lot. One time I remember we were talking about Vietnam, and she said something about how whether the war was bad or not, the men who were fighting it were still good men, and she talked about how her father was killed in Korea. And one time she said, 'If he had lived, I guess everything would be different.' "

"Different how?"

"She didn't say."

ELEVEN

I gave the car back to the Olin people a little after two. I stopped for a sandwich and a piece of pie and went through my notebook, trying to find a way that everything would connect with everything else.

Wendy Hanniford. She had a thing for older men, and if you wanted to you could run a trace on it all the way back to unresolved feelings for the father she never saw. At college she realized her own power and had affairs with professors. Then one of them fell too hard for her and a wheel came off, and by the time it was over she was out of school and on her own in New York.

There were plenty of older men in New York. One of them took her to Miami Beach. The same one, or another, provided her with a job reference when she rented her apartment. And all along the line there must have been plenty of older men to take her to dinner, to slip her twenty dollars for taxi fare, to leave twenty or thirty or fifty dollars on the bureau.

She had never needed a roommate. She had subsidized Marcia Maisel, asking considerably less than half the rent. It was likely she had subsidized Richie Vanderpoel as well, and it was just as likely she had taken him as a roommate for the same reason she'd taken Marcia in, the same reason she had wanted Marcia to stick around.

Because it was a lonely world, and she had always lived alone in it with only her father's ghost for company. The men she got, the men she was drawn to, were men who belonged to other women and who went home to them when they were through with her. She wanted someone in that Bethune Street apartment who didn't want to take her to bed. Someone who would just be good company. First Marcia—and hadn't Wendy perhaps been a little disappointed when Marcia agreed to go along on dates with her? I guessed that she had, because at the same time that she gained a companion on dates she lost a companion who had been not of that brittle world but of a piece with the innocence Marcia had sensed in Wendy herself.

Then Richie, who had probably made an even better companion. Richie, a timid and reticent homosexual, who had improved the decor and cooked the gourmet meals and made a home for her while he kept his clothes in the living room and spent his nights on the convertible couch. And she in turn had provided Richie with a home. She'd given him a woman's companionship without posing the sexual challenge another woman might have constituted. He moved in with her and out of the gay bars.

I paid the check and left, heading down Broadway and back to the hotel. A panhandler, red-eyed and ragged, blocked my path. He wanted to know if I had any spare change. I shook my head and kept walking at him, and he scuttled out of the way. He looked as though he wanted to tell me to fuck myself if only he had the nerve.

How much deeper did I want to go with it? I could fly to Indiana and make a nuisance of myself on the campus where Wendy had learned to define her role in life. I could easily enough learn the name of the professor whose affair with her had had such dramatic results. I could find that professor, whether he was still at that school or not. He would talk to me. I could make him talk to me. I could track down other professors who had slept with her, other students who had known her.

But what could they tell me that I didn't know? I was not writing her biography. I was trying to capture enough of the essence of her so that I could go to Cale Hanniford and tell him who she was and how she got that way. I probably had enough to do a fair job of that already. I wouldn't find out much more in Indiana.

There was only one problem. In a very real sense, my arrangement with Hanniford was more than a dodge around the detective licensing laws and the income tax. The money he gave me was a gift, just as the money I'd give Koehler and Pankow and the postal clerk had been. And in return I was doing him a favor, just as they had done me favors. I was not working for him.

So I couldn't call it quits just because I had the answers to Cale Hanniford's questions. I had a question or two of my own, and I didn't have all the answers nailed down yet. I had most of it, or thought I did, but there were still a few blank spaces and I wanted to fill them in.

• • •

Vincent was at the desk when I walked in. He had given me a hard time awhile back, and he still wasn't sure how I felt about him. I'd just given him a ten for Christmas, which should have clued him in that I harbored no ill feelings, but he still had a tendency to cringe when I approached. He cringed a little now, then handed me my room key and a slip of paper that informed me Kenny had called. There was a number where I could reach him.

I called it from my room. "Ah, Matthew," he said. "How nice of you to call."

"What's the problem?"

"There is no problem. I'm just busy enjoying a day off. It was that or go to jail, and I'm none too fond of jails. I'm sure they would bring back unpleasant memories."

"I don't follow you."

"Am I being terribly oblique? I talked to the good Lieutenant Koehler, just as you suggested. Sinthia's is scheduled to be raided sometime this evening. Forewarned is forearmed, to coin a phrase, so I took the precaution of engaging one of my bartenders to mind the store this afternoon and evening."

"Does he know what's coming?"

"I'm not diabolical, Matthew. He knows he'll be locked up. He also knows that he'll be bailed out in nothing flat and charges will be dropped in short order. And he knows he'll be fifty dollars richer for the experience. Personally, I wouldn't suffer the indignity of an arrest for ten times that sum, but different strokes for different folks, to coin another phrase. Your Lieutenant Koehler was most cooperative, I might add, except he wanted a

119

hundred dollars instead of the fifty you suggested. I don't suppose I ought to have tried bargaining with him?''

"Probably not.''

"That's what I thought. Well, if it works out, the price is a pittance. I hope you don't mind that I mentioned your name?''

"Not at all.''

"It seemed to afford me a certain degree of entrée. But it leaves me owing you a favor, and I'm delighted to be able to discharge my obligation forthwith.''

"You got a line on Richie Vanderpoel?''

"I did indeed. I devoted quite a few hours to asking pertinent questions at an after-hours place. The one on Houston Street?''

"I don't know it.''

"Quite my favorite blind pig. I'll take you there some night if you'd like.''

"We'll see. What did you find out?''

"Ah, let me see. What *did* I find out? I talked to three gentlemen who were willing to remember taking our bright-eyed boy home for milk and cookies. I also talked to a few others who I would happily swear did the same, but their memories were clouded, sad to say. It seems I was quite right in thinking that he hadn't been hustling a buck. He never asked anyone for money, and one chap said he'd tried to press a few bob on Richie for cabfare home and the lad wouldn't take it. Sterling character, wouldn't you say?''

"I would.''

"And all too rare in this day and age. That's it in the hard-fact department. The rest is impressions, but I gather that's what you're most interested in.''

"Yes."

"Well, it seems Richard wasn't terribly sexy."

"Huh?"

He sighed. "The dear boy didn't like it much and wasn't terribly good at it. I gather it wasn't just a matter of nerves, although he does seem to have been a nervous and apprehensive sort. It was more a matter of being uncomfortable with the whole thing and getting blessed little pleasure out of sex itself. And he retreated from intimacy. He'd perform the dirty deed willingly enough, but he didn't want to have his hand held or his shoulder stroked. That's not unheard of, you know. There's a species of faggot that craves the sex but can't stand the closeness. All their friends are doomed to stay strangers. But he didn't seem to enjoy the sex all that much, either."

"Interesting."

"I thought you'd say so. Also, once it was over, Richie was ever so anxious to be on his way. Not the sort to stay the night. Didn't even care to linger for coffee and brandy. Just wham-bam-thank-you-sir. And no interest in a repeat performance at a later date. One chap really wanted to see the boy again, not because the sex was good, as it wasn't, but because he was intrigued. Thought he might pierce that grim exterior given another opportunity. Richie would have none of it. Didn't even want to speak to anyone once he'd shared a pillow with him."

"These three men—"

"No names, Matthew. I has me code of ethics, I does."

"I'm not interested in their names. I just wondered if they ran to type."

"In what way?"

"Age. Are they all about the same age?"

"More or less."

"All fifty or more?"

"How did you know?"

"Just a guess."

"Well, it's a good one. I'd place them all between fifty or sixty. And they look their years, poor devils, unlike those of us who have bathed in the fountain of youth."

"It all fits."

"How?"

"Too complicated to explain."

"Meaning bugger off? *I* don't mind. The mere satisfaction of knowing I've been helpful, Matthew, is reward enough for me. It's not as though I'd want a story to tell my granchildren in my old age."

TWELVE

Eddie Koehler was away from his desk. I left a message for him to call me back, then went downstairs and picked up a paper at the newsstand in the lobby. I had worked my way through to Dear Abby when the phone rang.

He thanked me for sending Kenny to him, his voice wary as he did so. I wasn't on the force, and he shouldn't have to kick any of it back to me.

I set his mind at rest. "You could do me a little favor in return. You can find someone to make a few phone calls or look in the right books. I could probably do it myself, but it would take me three times as long."

I spelled it out for him. It was an easy way for him to balance the books with me, and he was glad to grab it. He said he'd get back to me, and I told him I'd hang around and wait for his call.

It came almost exactly an hour later. J.J. Cottrell, Inc., had had offices in the Kleinhans Building at William and Pine. The firm had published a Wall Street tip sheet for about a dozen years, going out of business at the time of the proprietor's death. The proprietor had been one Arnold P. Leverett, and he'd died two and a half years ago. There had been no one named Cottrell connected with the firm.

I thanked him and rang off. That rounded things out neatly enough. I hadn't been able to find a Cottrell because there had never been one in the first place. It was reasonable to assume that Leverett had played some sort of role in Wendy Hanniford's life, but whether it had been a large or a small role was now no longer material. The man couldn't be reached for comment without the services of a medium.

For the hell of it I put through a call to the Eden Roc and got the manager again. He remembered me. I asked him if he could check the same register for Leverett, and it didn't take him as long this time because he knew right away where to find the records. Not too surprisingly, his records indicated that Mr. and Mrs. Arnold P. Leverett had been guests of the Eden Roc from the fourteenth to the twentieth of September.

So I had the name of one of the men in her life. If Leverett had left a widow, I could go and annoy her, but it would be hard to think up a less purposeful act. What I'd really accomplished was more negative than positive. I could now forget about tracing the man who had taken her to Florida, and I could quit wondering who in hell J.J. Cottrell was. He wasn't a person, he was a corporation, and he was out of business.

I went around the corner to Armstrong's and sat at the bar. It had already been a long day, and the drive to Mamaroneck and back had tired me more than I realized. I figured on spending the rest of the night on that barstool, balancing coffee and bourbon until it was late enough to go back to my room and go to sleep.

It didn't work out that way. After two drinks I thought of something to do and couldn't talk myself out of doing it. It looked to be a waste of time, but everything was a waste of time, one way or another, and evidently something in me demanded that I waste my time in this particular fashion.

And it wasn't such a waste after all.

I caught a cab on Ninth and listened to the driver bitch about the price of gasoline. It was all a conspiracy, he said, and he explained just how it was structured. The big oil companies were all owned by Zionists and by cutting off the oil they would turn public opinion in favor of the United States teaming up with Israel to seize the oil-rich Arab territory. He even found a way to tie it all in with the assassination of Kennedy. I forget which Kennedy.

"It's my own theory," he said. "Whaddaya think of it?"

"It's a theory."

"Makes sense, doesn't it?"

"I don't know that much about the subject."

"Yeah, sure. That's the American public for you. Nobody knows from nothing. Nobody cares. Take a poll on a subject, any subject, and half the people got no opinion. No opinion! That's why the country's going to hell."

"I figured there was a reason."

He let me out in front of the library at Forty-second and Fifth. I walked between the stone lions and up the stairs to the Microfilm Room. I checked my notebook for the date of Arnold P. Leverett's death and filled out a slip. A sad-eyed girl in jeans and a plaid blouse brought me the appropriate spool of film.

I threaded it into the scanner and started going through it. It's almost impossible to go through old issues of the *Times* on microfilm without getting sidetracked. Other stories catch your eye and waste your time. But I forced myself to locate the proper obituary page and read the article on Arnold Philip Leverett.

He didn't warrant much space. Four paragraphs, and nothing tremendously exciting in any of them. He had died of a heart attack at his home in Port Washington. He had left a wife and three children. He had gone to various schools and worked for various stockbrokers before leaving in 1959 to start his own Wall Street newsletter, *Cottrell's Weekly Analyzer*. He had been fifty-eight years old at the time of his death. The last fact was the only one that could possibly be considered pertinent, and it only confirmed what I had already taken pretty much for granted.

I wonder what makes people think of things. Maybe some other story caught the corner of my eye and jogged something loose in my mind. I don't know what did it, and I wasn't even aware of it until I had already left the Microfilm Room and gone halfway down the stairs. Then I turned around and went back where I'd come from and got the *Times Index* for 1959.

That was the year Leverett started his tip sheet, so maybe that was what had triggered it. I looked through the *Index* and established that it was also the year in which Mrs. Martin Vanderpoel died.

I hadn't really expected to find an obituary. She had been a clergyman's wife, but he wasn't all that prominent, a minister with a small congregation out in the wilds of Brooklyn. I'd been looking for nothing more than a death notice, but there was a regular *Times* obit, and when I had the right spool in the scanner and ran down the page with her obituary on it, I knew why they'd thought she was worth the space.

Mrs. Martin Vanderpoel, the former Miss Frances Elizabeth Hegermann, had committed suicide. She had done so in the bathroom of the rectory of the First Reformed Church of Bay Ridge. She had slashed her wrists, and she had been discovered dead in the bathtub by her young son, Richard.

I went back to Armstrong's, but it was the wrong place for the mood I was in. I headed uptown on Ninth and kept going after it turned into Columbus Avenue. I hit a lot of bars, stopping for a quick drink whenever I got tired of walking. There are plenty of bars on Columbus Avenue.

I was looking for something but I didn't know what it was until I found it. I should have been able to tell in advance. I had had nights like this before, walking through bad streets, waiting for an opportunity to blow off some of the things that had been building up inside me.

I got the chance on Columbus somewhere in the high Eighties. I had left a bar with an Irish name and Spanish-speaking customers, and I was letting myself walk with the rolling gait that is the special property of drunks and sailors. I saw movement in a doorway ten or twelve yards ahead of me, but I kept right on walking, and when he came out of the doorway with a knife in his hand, I knew I'd been looking for him for hours.

He said, "Come on, come on, gimme your money."

He wasn't a junkie. Everybody thinks they're all junkies, but they're not. Junkies break into apartments when nobody's home and take television sets and typewriters, small things they can turn into quick cash. Not more than one mugger out of five has a real jones. The other four do it because it beats working.

And it lets them know how tough they are.

He made sure I could see the knife blade. We were in the shadows, but the blade still caught a little light and flashed wickedly at me. It was a kitchen knife, wooden handle, six or seven inches of blade.

I said, "Just take it easy."

"Let's see that fucking money."

"Sure," I said. "Just take it easy with the knife. Knives make me nervous."

I suppose he was about nineteen or twenty. He'd had a fierce case of acne not too many years ago, and his cheeks and chin were pitted. I moved toward my inside breast pocket, and in an easy, rolling motion I dropped one shoulder, pivoted on my right heel, and kicked his wrist with my left foot. The knife sailed out of his hand.

He went for it and that was a mistake because it landed behind him and he had to scramble for it. He should have done one of two things. He should have come straight at me or he should have turned around and run away but instead he went for the knife and that was the wrong thing to do.

He never got within ten feet of it. He was off balance and scrambling, and I got a hand on his shoulder and spun him like a top. I threw a right, my hand open, and I caught him with the heel of my hand right under his nose. He yelped and put both hands to his face, and I hit him three or four times in the belly. When he folded up I cupped my hands on the back of his head and brought my knee up while I was bringing his head down.

The impact was good and solid. I let go of him, and he stood in a dazed crouch, his legs bent at right angles at the knees. His body didn't know whether to straighten up or fall down. I took his chin in my hand and shoved, and that made the decision for him. He went up and over and sprawled on his back and stayed that way.

I found a thick roll of bills in the right-hand pocket of his jeans. He wasn't looking to buy milk for his hungry brothers and sisters, not this one. He'd been carrying just under two hundred dollars on his hip. I tucked a single back in his pocket for the subway and added the rest to my wallet. He lay there without moving and watched the whole operation. I don't think he believed it was really happening.

I got down on one knee. I picked up his right hand in my left hand and put my face close to his. His eyes were wide and he was frightened, and I was glad because I wanted him to be frightened. I wanted him to know just what fear was and just how it felt.

I said, "Listen to me. These are hard, tough streets, and you are not hard enough or tough enough. You better get a straight job because you can't make it out here, you're too soft for it. You think it's easy out here, but it's harder than you ever knew, and now's your chance to learn it.''

I bent the fingers of his right hand back one at a time until they broke. Just the four fingers. I left his thumb alone. He didn't scream or anything. I suppose the terror blocked the pain.

I took his knife along with me and dropped it in the first sewer I came to. Then I walked the two blocks to Broadway and caught a cab home.

THIRTEEN

I don't think I actually slept at all.

I got out of my clothes and into bed. I closed my eyes and slipped into the kind of dream you can have without being entirely asleep, aware that it was a dream, my consciousness standing off to one side and watching the dream like a jaded critic at the theater. Then a batch of things came together, and I knew I wouldn't be able to sleep and didn't want to, anyway.

So I ran the shower as hot as it gets and stood by the side of the tub with the bathroom door closed to create an improvised steam bath. I sweated exhaustion and alcohol out of my system for half an hour or so. Then I lowered the temperature of the shower enough to make it bearable and stood under it. I finished with a minute under an ice-cold spray. I don't know if it's really good for you. I think it's just Spartan.

I dried off and put on a clean suit. I sat on the bed and picked up the telephone. Allegheny turned out to have the flight I wanted. It was leaving LaGuardia at five forty-five and would get me where I was going a little after seven. I booked a round-trip ticket, return open.

The Childs' at Fifty-eighth and Eighth stays open all night. I had corned beef hash and eggs and a lot of black coffee.

It was very close to five o'clock when I got into the back of a Checker cab and told the driver to take me to the airport.

The flight had a stop in Albany. That's what took it so long. It touched down there on schedule. A few people got off, and a few other people got on, and the pilot put us into the air again. We never had time to level off on the second lap; we began our descent as soon as we stopped climbing. He bounced us around a little on the Utica runway, but it was nothing to complain about.

"Have a good day," the stewardess said. "Take care now."

Take care.

It seems to me that people have only been saying that phrase on parting for the past few years or so. All of a sudden everyone started to say it, as if the whole country abruptly recognized that ours is a world which demands caution.

I intended to take care. I wasn't too sure about having a good day.

By the time I got from the airport into Utica itself, it was around seven thirty. A few minutes of twelve I called Cale Hanniford at his office. No one answered.

I tried his home and his wife answered. I gave my name and she told me hers. "Mr. Scudder," she said tentatively. "Are you, uh, making any progress?"

"Things are coming along," I said.

"I'll get Cale for you."

When he came on the line I told him I wanted to see him.

"I see. Something you don't want to go into over the telephone?"

"Something like that."

"Well, can you come to Utica? It would be inconvenient for me to come to New York unless it's absolutely necessary, but you could fly up this afternoon or possibly tomorrow. It's not a long flight."

"I know. I'm in Utica right now."

"Oh?"

"I'm in a Rexall drugstore at the corner of Jefferson and Mohawk. You could pick me up and we could go over to your office."

"Certainly. Fifteen minutes?"

"Fine."

I recognized his Lincoln and was crossing the sidewalk to it as he pulled up in front of the drugstore. I opened the door and got in next to him. Either he wore a suit around the house as a matter of course or he had taken the trouble to put one on for the occasion. The suit was dark blue with an unobtrusive stripe.

"You should have let me know you were coming," he said. "I could have picked you up at the airport."

"This way I had a chance to see something of your city."

"It's not a bad place. Probably very quiet by New York standards. Though that's not necessarily a bad thing."

"No, it's not."

"Ever been here before?"

"Once, and that was years ago. The local police had picked up someone we wanted, so I came up to take him back to New York with me. I took the train that trip."

"How was your flight today?"

"All right."

He was dying to ask me why I had dropped in on him like this, but he had manners. You didn't discuss business at lunch until the coffee was poured, and we wouldn't discuss our business until we were in his office. The Hanniford Drugs warehouse was on the western edge of town, and he had picked me up right in the heart of the downtown area. We managed small talk on the ride out. He pointed out things he thought might interest me, and I put on a show of being mildly interested. Then we were at the warehouse. They worked a five-day week and there were no other cars around, just a couple of idle trucks. He pulled the Lincoln to a stop next to a loading dock and led me up a ramp and inside. We walked down a hallway to his office. He turned on the overhead lights, pointed me to a chair, and seated himself behind his desk.

"Well," he said.

I didn't feel tired. It occurred to me that I ought to, no sleep, a lot of booze the night before. But I didn't feel tired. Not eager, either, but not tired.

I said, "I came to report. I know as much about your daughter as I'll ever know, and it's as much as you need to know. I could spend more of my time and your money, but I don't see the point."

"It didn't take you very long."

His tone was neutral, and I wondered how he meant it. Was he admiring my efficiency or annoyed that his two thousand dollars had only purchased five days of my time?

I said, "It took long enough. I don't know that it would have taken any less time if you had given me everything in the beginning. Probably not. It would have made things a little easier for me, though."

"I don't understand."

"I can understand why you didn't. You felt I had all I needed to know. If I had just been looking for facts you might have been right, but I was looking for facts that would make up a picture, and I'd have done better knowing everything in front." He was puzzled, and the heavy dark eyebrows were elevated above the top rims of his glasses. I said, "The reason I didn't let you know I was coming was that I had some things to do in Utica. I caught a dawn flight up here, Mr. Hanniford. I spent about five hours learning things you could have told me five days ago."

"What sort of things?"

"I went to a few places. The Bureau of Vital Statistics in City Hall. The *Times-Sentinel* offices. The police station."

"I didn't hire you to ask questions here in Utica."

"You didn't hire me at all, Mr. Hanniford. You married your wife on—well, I don't have to tell you the date. It was a first marriage for both of you."

He didn't say anything. He took his glasses off and put them on the desk in front of him.

"You might have told me Wendy was illegitimate."

"Why? She didn't know it herself."

"Are you sure of that?"

"Yes."

"I'm not." I drew a breath. "There were two U.S. Marines from the Utica area killed in the Inchon landing. One of them was black, so I ruled him out. The other was named Robert Blohr. He was married. Was he also Wendy's father?"

"Yes."

"I'm not trying to pick scabs, Mr. Hanniford. I think Wendy knew she was illegitimate. And it's possible that it doesn't matter whether she did or not."

He stood up and walked to the window. I sat there wondering whether Wendy had known about her father and decided it was ten-to-one that she had. He was the chief character in her personal mythology, and she had spent all her life looking for an incarnation of him. The ambivalence of her feelings about the man seemed to derive from some knowledge over and above what she had been told by Hanniford and her mother.

He stayed at the window for a time. Then he turned and looked thoughtfully at me. "Perhaps I should have told you," he said finally. "I didn't conceal it on purpose. That is, I gave little thought at the time to Wendy's . . . illegitimacy. That's been a completely closed chapter for so many years that it never occurred to me to mention it."

"I can understand that."

"You said you had a report to make," he said. He returned to his chair and sat down. "Go ahead, Scudder."

I started all the way back in Indiana. Wendy at college, not interested in boys her own age, interested always in older men. She had had affairs with her professors, most of them probably casual liaisons, one at least other than casual, at least on the man's part. He had wanted to leave his wife. The wife had taken pills, perhaps in a genuine suicide attempt, perhaps as a grandstand play to save her marriage. And perhaps she herself hadn't known which.

"At any rate, there was a scandal of sorts. The whole campus was aware of it, whether or not it became officially a matter of record. That explains why Wendy dropped out of school a couple of months short of graduation. There was really no way she could stay there."

"Of course not."

"It also explains why the school wasn't desperately concerned that she had disappeared. I'd wondered about that. From what you said, their attitude was fairly casual. Evidently they wanted to let you know she was gone but weren't prepared to tell you why she had left, but they knew she had good reasons to leave and weren't concerned about her physical well-being."

"I see."

"She went to New York, as you know. She became involved with older men almost immediately. One of them took her to Miami. I could give you his name, but it doesn't matter. He died a couple of years ago. It's hard to tell now just how big a role he played in Wendy's life, but in addition to taking her to Miami he let her use his name when she applied for her apartment. She put his firm down as her employer, and he backed her up when the rental agent called."

"Did he pay her rent?"

"It's possible. Whether he paid all or part of her support at the time is something only he could tell you, and there's no way to ask him. If you want my guess, her involvement with him was not an exclusive one."

"There were other men in her life at the same time?"

"I think so. This particular man was married and lived in the suburbs with his family. I doubt that he could have spent all that much time with her even if either of them wanted it that way. And I have a feeling she was leery of getting too involved with one man. It must have shaken her a great deal when the professor's wife took the pills. If he was sufficiently infatuated with her to leave his wife for her, she was probably committed to him herself, or at least thought she was. After that fell apart she was careful not to invest too much of herself in any one man."

"So she saw a lot of men."

"Yes."

"And took money from them."

"Yes."

"You know that for a fact? Or is it conjecture?"

"It's fact." I told him a little about Marcia Maisel and how she had gradually become aware of the manner in which Wendy was supporting herself. I didn't add that Marcia had tried the profession on for size.

He lowered his head, and a little of the starch went out of his shoulders. "So the newspapers were accurate," he said. "She was a prostitute."

"A kind of prostitute."

"What does that mean? It's like pregnancy, isn't it? Either you are or you aren't."

"I think it's more like honesty."

"Oh?"

"Some people are more honest than others."

"I always thought honesty was unequivocal, too."

"Maybe it is. I think there are different levels."

"And there are different levels of prostitution?"

"I'd say so. Wendy wasn't walking the streets. She wasn't turning one trick after another, wasn't handing her money over to a pimp."

"Isn't that what the Vanderpoel boy was?"

"No. I'll get to him." I closed my eyes for a moment. I opened them and said, "There's no way to know this for certain, but I doubt that Wendy set out to be a prostitute. She probably took money from quite a few men before she could pin that label on herself."

"I don't follow you."

"Let's say a man took her out to dinner, brought her home, wound up going to bed with her. On his way out the door he might hand her a twenty-dollar bill. He'd say something like, 'I'd like to send you a big bouquet of flowers or buy you a present, but why not take the money and pick out something you like?' Maybe she tried not to take the money the first few times this happened. Later on she'd learn to expect it."

"I see."

"It wouldn't be long before she would start getting telephone calls from men she hadn't met. A lot of men like to pass girls' phone numbers around. Sometimes it's an act of charity. Other times they think they enhance their own image this way. 'She's a great kid, she's not exactly a hooker, but slip her a few bucks afterward because she doesn't have a job, you know, and it's tough for a girl to make it in the big city.' So you wake up one morning and realize that you're a prostitute, at least according to the dictionary definition of the term, but by then you're used to the way you're living and it doesn't seem unnatural to you. As far as I can determine, she never asked for money. She never saw more than one man during an evening. She turned down dates if she didn't like the man involved. She would even plead a fake headache if she met a man for dinner and decided she didn't want to sleep with him. So she earned her money that way, but she wasn't in it for the money.''

"You mean she enjoyed it."

"She certainly found it tolerable. She wasn't kidnapped by white slavers. She could have found a job if she wanted one. She could have come home to Utica, or called up and asked for money. Are you asking if she was a nymphomaniac? I don't know the answer to that, but I'd be inclined to doubt it. I think she was compelled.''

"How?"

I stood up and moved closer to his desk. It was dark mahogany and looked at least fifty years old. Its top was orderly. There was a blotter in a tooled leather holder, a two-tiered in-and-out box, a spindle, a pair of framed photographs. He watched me pick up both photographs and look at them. One showed a woman about forty, her eyes out of focus, an uncertain smile on her face. I sensed that the expression was not uncharacteristic. The other photo was of Wendy, her hair medium in length, her eyes bright, and her teeth shiny enough to sell toothpaste.

"When was this taken?"

"High school graduation."

"And this is your wife?"

"Yes. I don't know when that was taken. Six or seven years ago, I would guess."

"I don't see a resemblance."

"No. Wendy favored her father."

"Blohr."

"Yes. I never met him. I'm told she resembled him. I couldn't say one way or the other, on the basis of my own knowledge, but I'm told she does. Did."

I returned Mrs. Hanniford's photo to its place on his desk. I looked into Wendy's eyes. We had become too intimate these past few days, she and I. I probably knew more about her than she might have wanted me to know.

"You said you thought she was compelled."

I nodded.

"By what?"

I put the photo back where it belonged. I watched Hanniford try not to meet Wendy's eyes. He didn't manage it. He looked into them and winced.

I said, "I'm not a psychologist, a psychiatrist, any of those things. I'm just a man who used to be a cop."

"I know that."

"I can make guesses. I'd guess she could never stop looking for Daddy. She wanted to be somebody's daughter, and they kept wanting to fuck her. And that was all right with her because that was what Daddy was, he was a man who took Mommy to bed and got her pregnant and then went away to Korea and was never heard from again. He was somebody who was married to somebody else, and that was all right, because the men she was attracted to were always married to somebody else. It could get very hairy looking for

Daddy because if you weren't careful he might like you too much and Mommy might take a lot of pills and it would be time for you to go away. That's why it was safer all around if Daddy gave you money. Then it was all on a cash-and-carry basis and Daddy wouldn't flip out over you and Mommy wouldn't take pills and you could stay where you were, you wouldn't have to leave. I'm not a psychiatrist and I don't know if this is the way it works in textbooks or not. I never read the textbooks and I never met Wendy. I didn't get inside of her life until her life was over. I kept trying to get into her life and I kept getting into her death instead. Do you have anything to drink?"

"Pardon me?"

"Do you have anything to drink? Like bourbon."

"Oh. I think there's a bottle of something or other."

How could you not know whether or not you had any liquor around?

"Get it."

His face went through some interesting changes. He started off wondering who the hell I thought I was to order him around, and then he realized that it was immaterial, and then he got up and went over to a cabinet and opened a door.

"It's Canadian Club," he announced.

"Fine."

"I don't believe I have anything to mix it with."

"Good. Just bring the bottle and a glass." And if you don't have a glass, that's all right, sir.

He brought the bottle and a water tumbler and watched with clinical interest as I poured whiskey until the glass was two-thirds full. I drank off about half of it and put the glass down on top of his desk. Then I picked it up quickly because it might have left a ring otherwise, and I made hesitant motions and he decoded them and handed me a couple of memo slips that could serve as a coaster.

"Scudder?"

"What?"

"Do you suppose a psychiatrist could have helped her?"

"I don't know. Maybe she went to one. I couldn't find anything in her apartment to suggest that she did, but it's possible. I think she was helping herself."

"By living the way she did?"

"Uh-huh. Her life was a fairly stable one. It may not look like it from the outside, but I think it was. That's why she carried the Maisel girl as a roommate. It's also why she hooked up with Vanderpoel. Her apartment had a very settled feel to it. Well-chosen furniture. A place to live in. I think the men in her life represented a stage she was working her way through, and I would guess that she consciously saw it that way. The men represented physical and emotional survival for the time being, and I think she anticipated reaching a point where she wouldn't need them anymore."

I drank some more whiskey. It was a little sweet for my taste, and a little too smooth, but it went down well enough.

I said, "In some ways I learned more about Richie Vanderpoel than I did about Wendy. One of the people I talked to said all ministers' sons are crazy. I don't know that that's true, but I think most of them must have a hard time of it. Richie's father is a very uptight type. Stern, cold. I doubt that he ever showed the boy much in the way of warmth. Richie's mother killed herself when he was six years old. No brothers or sisters, just the kid and his father and a dried-up housekeeper in a rectory that could double as a mausoleum. He grew up with mixed-up feelings about both of his parents. His feelings in that area complemented Wendy's pretty closely. That's why they were so good for each other."

"Good for each other!"

"Yes."

"For God's sake, he killed her!"

"They were good for each other. She was a woman he wasn't afraid of, and he was a man she couldn't mistake for her father. They were able to have a domestic life together that gave them both a measure of security they hadn't had before. And there was no sexual relationship to complicate things."

"They didn't sleep together?"

I shook my head. "Richie was homosexual. At least he'd been functioning as a homosexual before he moved in with your daughter. He didn't like it much, wasn't comfortable about it. Wendy gave him a chance to get away from that life. He could life with a woman without having to prove his manhood because she didn't want him as a lover. After he met her he stopped making the rounds of the gay bars. And I think she stopped seeing men in the evenings. I couldn't prove it, but earlier she had been getting taken out for dinner several nights a week. The kitchen in her apartment was fully stocked when I saw it. I think Richie cooked dinner for the two of them just about every night. I told you a few minutes ago that I thought Wendy was working things out. I think both of them were working things out together. Maybe they would have started sleeping together eventually. Maybe Wendy would have stopped seeing men professionally and gone out and taken a job. I'm just guessing, that's all any of this is, but I'd take the guess a little further. I think they would have gotten married eventually, and they might even have made it work."

"That's very hypothetical."

"I know."

"You make it sound as though they were in love."

"I don't know that they were in love. I don't think there's any doubt that they loved each other."

He picked up his glasses, put them on, took them off again. I poured more whiskey in my glass and took a small sip of it. He sat for a long while, looking at his hands. Every now and then he looked up at the two photographs on top of his desk.

Finally he said, "Then why did he kill her?"

"No way to answer that. He didn't have any memory of the act, and the whole scene got mixed up with memories of his mother's death. Anyway, that's not your question."

"It's not?"

"Of course not. What you want to know is how much of it was your fault."

He didn't say anything.

"Something happened the last time you saw your daughter. Do you want to tell me about it?"

He didn't want to, not a whole hell of a lot, and it took him a few minutes to get warmed up. He talked vaguely about the sort of child she had been, very bright and warm and affectionate, and about how much he had loved her.

Then he said, "When she was, it's hard to remember, but I think she must have been eight years old. Eight or nine. She would always sit on my lap and give me hugs and . . . hugs and kisses, and she would squirm around a little, and—"

He had to stop for a minute. I didn't say anything.

"One day, I don't know why it happened, but one day she was on my lap, and I—oh, Christ."

"Take your time."

"I got excited. Physically excited."

"It happens."

"Does it?" His face looked like something from a stained-glass window. "I couldn't . . . couldn't even think about it. I was so disgusted with myself. I loved her the way you love a daughter, at least I had always thought that was what I felt for her, and to find myself responding to her sexually—"

"I'm no expert, Mr. Hanniford, but I think it's a very natural thing. Just a physical response. Some people get erections from riding on trains."

"This was more than that."

"Maybe."

"It was, Scudder. I was terrified of what I saw in myself. Terrified of what it could lead to, the harm it could have for Wendy. And so I made a conscious decision that day. I stopped being so close to her." He lowered his eyes. "I withdrew. I made myself limit my affection for her, the affection I expressed, that is. Maybe the affection I felt as well. There was less hugging and kissing and cuddling. I was determined not to let that one occasion repeat itself."

He sighed, fixed his eyes on mine. "How much of this did you guess at, Scudder?"

"A little of it. I thought it might even have gone farther than that."

"I'm not an animal."

"People do things you wouldn't believe. And they aren't always animals. What happened the last time you saw Wendy?"

"I've never told anyone about this. Why do I have to tell you?"

"You don't. But you want to."

"Do I?" He sighed again. "She was home from college. Everything was the way it had always been, but there was something about her that was different. I suppose she had already established a pattern of getting involved with older men."

"Yes."

"She came home late one night. She'd gone out alone. Perhaps she let someone pick her up, I don't know." He closed his eyes and looked back at that evening. "I was awake when she came home. I wasn't purposely waiting up for her. My wife had gone to sleep early, and I had a book I wanted to read. Wendy came home around one or two in the morning. She'd been drinking. She wasn't reeling, but she was at least slightly drunk.

"I saw a side of her I had never seen before. She . . . she propositioned me."

"Just like that?"

"She asked me if I wanted to fuck. She said . . . obscene things. Described acts she wanted to perform with me. She tried to grab me."

"What did you do?"

"I slapped her."

"I see."

"I told her she was drunk. I told her to go upstairs and get to bed. I don't know if the slap sobered her, but a shadow passed over her face and she turned away without a word and climbed the stairs. I didn't know what to do. I thought perhaps I ought to go to her and tell her it was all right, that we would just forget about it. In the end I did nothing. I sat up for another hour or so, then went to bed myself." He looked up. "And in the morning we both pretended nothing had happened. Neither of us ever referred to the incident again."

I drank what was in my glass. It all meshed now, every bit of it.

"The reason I didn't go to her . . . I was sickened by the way she acted. Disgusted. But something in me was . . . excited."

I nodded.

"I'm not sure I trusted myself to go to her room that night, Scudder."

"Nothing would have happened."

"How do you know that?"

"Everybody has mean little places inside himself. It's the ones who aren't aware of them who fly off the handle. You were able to see what was happening. That made you capable of keeping a lid on it."

"Maybe."

After a while I said, "I don't think you have much to blame yourself for. It seems to me that everything was already set in motion before you were in a position to do anything about it. It wasn't a one-sided thing when you responded physically to Wendy squirming around on your lap. She was behaving seductively, although I'm sure she didn't realize it at the time. It all fits together—competing with her mother, trying to find Daddy hiding inside every older man she found attractive. Lots of girls try to seduce professors, you know, and most professors learn to be very good at discouraging that sort of thing. Wendy had a pretty high success ratio. She was evidently very good at it."

"It's funny."

"What is?"

"Earlier you made her sound like a victim. Now she sounds like a villain."

"Everybody's both."

Neither of us had very much to say on the way out to the airport. He seemed more relaxed than before, but I had no way of knowing how much of that was just on the surface. If I'd done him any good, I'd done so less by what I had found out for him than by what I'd made him tell me. There were priests and psychiatrists who would have listened to him, and they probably would have done him more good than I did, but I'd been elected instead.

At one point I said, "Whatever blame you decide to assign yourself, keep one thing in mind. Wendy was in the process of turning out all right. I don't know how long it would have taken her to find a cleaner way of making a living, but I doubt it would have been much more than a year."

"You can't be certain of that."

"I certainly can't prove it."

"That makes it worse, doesn't it? It makes it more tragic."

"It makes it more tragic. I don't know if that's better or worse."

"What? Oh, I see. That's an interesting distinction."

I went to the Allegheny desk. There was a flight to New York within the hour, and I checked in for it. When I turned around, Hanniford was standing next to me with a check in his hand. I asked him what it was for. He said I hadn't mentioned more money and he didn't know what constituted a fair payment, but he was pleased with the job I had done for him and he wanted to give me a bonus.

I didn't know what was fair payment, either. But I remembered what I had told Lewis Pankow. When somebody hands you money, you take it. I took it.

I didn't get around to unfolding it until I was on the plane. It was for a thousand dollars. I'm still not sure why he gave it to me.

FOURTEEN

In my hotel room I opened a paperback dictionary of saints and flipped through it. I found myself reading about St. Mary Goretti, who was born in Italy in 1890. When she was twelve a young man began making overtures to her. Eventually he attempted to ravish her and threatened to kill her if she resisted. She did, and he did, stabbing her over and over again with his knife. She died within twenty-four hours.

After eight years of unrepentant imprisonment her murderer had a change of heart, I learned. At the end of twenty-seven years he was released, and on Christmas Day, 1937, he contrived to receive Communion side by side with Mary's widowed mother. He has since been cited as an example by those who advocate the abolition of capital punishment.

I always find something interesting in that book.

I went next door for dinner but didn't have

much appetite. The waiter offered to put my left-over steak in a doggie bag. I told him not to bother.

So I went around the corner to Armstrong's and wound up at the corner table in back where it had all started just a few days ago. Cale Hanniford walked into my life on Tuesday, and now it was Saturday. It seemed as though it had been a lot longer than that.

It had started on Tuesday as far as I was concerned, but it had in fact started a lot earlier than that, and I sipped bourbon and coffee and wondered how far you could trace it back. At some point or other it had probably become inevitable, but I didn't know just when that point was. There was a day when Richie Vanderpoel and Wendy Hanniford met each other, and that had to be a turning point of one sort or another, but maybe their separate ends had been charted far in advance of that date and their meeting only arranged that they would happen to one another. Maybe it went a lot further back, to Robert Blohr dying in Korea and Margaret Vanderpoel opening her veins in her bathtub.

Maybe it was Eve's fault, messing around with apples. Dangerous thing, giving humanity the knowledge of good and evil. And the capacity to make the wrong choice more often than not.

"Buy a lady a drink?"

I looked up. It was Trina, dressed in civilian clothes and wearing a smile that faded as she studied my face. "Hey," she said. "Where *were* you?"

"Chasing private thoughts."

"Want to be alone?"

"That's the last thing I want. Did you say something about buying you a drink?"

"It was an idea I had, yes."

I flagged the waiter and ordered a stinger for her and another of the same for myself. She talked about a couple of strange customers she'd had the night before. We coasted through a few rounds on small talk, and then she reached out a hand and touched the tip of my chin with her finger.

"Hey."

"Hey?"

"Hey, you're in a bad way. Troubles?"

"I had a rotten day. I flew upstate and had a conversation that wasn't much fun."

"The business you were telling me about the other night?"

"Was I talking about it with you? Yes, I guess I was."

"Feel like talking about it now?"

"Maybe a little later."

"Sure."

We sat for a while, not saying much. The place was quiet as it often is on Saturdays. At one point two kids came in and walked over to the bar. I didn't recognize them.

"Matt, is something wrong?"

I didn't answer her. The bartender sold them a couple of six-packs and they left. I let out a breath I hadn't known I was holding.

"Matt?"

"Just a reflex. I thought the place was about to be held up. Put it down to nerves."

"Sure." Her hand covered mine. "Getting late," she said.

"Is it?"

"Kind of. Would you walk me home? It's just a couple of blocks."

She lived on the tenth floor of a new building on Fifty-sixth between Ninth and Tenth. The doorman roused himself enough to flash her a smile. "There's some booze," she told me, "and I can make better coffee than Jimmie can. Want to come up?"

"I'd like to."

Her apartment was a studio, one large room with an alcove that held a narrow bed. She showed me where to hang my coat and put on a stack of records. She said she'd put on some coffee, and I told her to forget about the coffee. She made drinks for both of us. She curled up on a red plush sofa and I sat in a frayed gray armchair.

"Nice place," I said.

"It's getting there. I want pictures for the walls and some of the furniture will have to be replaced eventually, but in the meantime it suits me."

"How long have you been here?"

"Since October. I lived uptown, and I hated taking cabs to and from work."

"Were you ever married, Trina?"

"For three years, almost. I've been divorced for four."

"Ever see your ex?"

"I don't even know what state he lives in. I think he's out on the Coast, but I'm not sure. Why?"

"No reason. You didn't have any kids?"

"No. He didn't want to. Then when things fell apart I was glad we didn't. You?"

"Two boys."

"That must be rough."

"I don't know. Sometimes, I guess."

"Matt? What would you have done if there was a holdup tonight?"

I thought it over. "Nothing, probably. Nothing I could do, really. Why?"

"You didn't see yourself when it was going on. You looked like a cat getting ready to spring."

"Reflexes."

"All those years being a cop."

"Something like that."

She lit a cigarette. I got the bottle and freshened our drinks. Then I was sitting on the couch next to her and telling her about Wendy and Richard, telling her just about all of it. I don't know whether it was her or the booze or a combination of the two, but it was suddenly very easy to talk about it, very important that I talk about it.

And I said, "The impossible thing was knowing how much to tell the man. He was afraid of what he might have done to her, either by limiting his affection for her or by behaving seductively toward her without knowing it himself. I can't find those answers any better than he can. But other things. The murder, the way his daughter died. How much of that was I supposed to tell him?"

"Well, he already knew all that, didn't he, Matt?"

"I guess he knew what he had to know."

"I don't follow you."

I started to say something, then let it go. I poured more booze in both our glasses. She looked at me. "Trying to get me drunk?"

"Trying to get us both drunk."

"Well, I think it's working. Matt—"

I said, "It's hard to know just how much a person has any right to do. I suppose I was on the force too long. Maybe I never should have left. Do you know about that?"

She averted her eyes. "Somebody said something once."

"Well, if that hadn't happened, would I have left anyway sooner or later? I always wonder about that. There was a great security in being a cop. I don't mean the job security, I mean the emotional security. There weren't as many questions, and the ones that came up were likely to have obvious answers, or at least they seemed obvious at the time.

"Let me tell you a story. This happened maybe ten years ago. Maybe twelve. It also happened in the Village and it involved a girl in her twenties. She was raped and murdered in her own apartment. Nylon stocking wrapped around her neck." Trina shuddered. "Now this one wasn't open-and-shut, there was nobody running around the streets with her blood on him. It was one of those cases where you just keep digging, you check out everybody who ever said boo to the girl, everybody in the building, everybody who knew her at work, every man who played any role whatsoever in her life. Christ, we must have talked to a couple of hundred people.

"Well, there was one guy I liked for it from the start. Big brawny son of a bitch, he was the super in the building she lived in. Ex-Navy man, got out on a bad-conduct discharge. We had a sheet on him. Two arrests for assault, both dropped when the complainants refused to press charges. Complainants in both cases were women.

"All that is enough reason to check him out down to the ground. Which we did. And the more I talked to him the more I knew the son of a bitch did it. Sometimes you just plain know.

"But he had himself covered. We had the time of death pinpointed to within an hour, and his wife was prepared to swear on a stack of bibles that he'd spent the entire day never out of her sight. And we had nothing on the other side of it, not one scrap of anything to place him in the girl's apartment at the time of the murder. Nothing at all. Not even a lousy fingerprint, and even if we did, it meant nothing because he was the super and he could have put his prints there fixing the plumbing or something. We had nothing, not a smell of anything, and the only reason we knew he did it was we simply knew, and no district attorney would dream of trying to run that by a grand jury.

"So we checked out everybody else who was vaguely possible. And of course we didn't get anywhere because there was nowhere to get, and the case wound up in the open file, which meant we knew it was never going to be closed out, which meant to all intents and purposes it was closed already because nobody would bother to look at it anymore."

I got to my feet, walked across the room. I said, "But we knew he did it, see, and it was driving us crazy. I don't know how many people get away with murder every year. A lot more than anyone realizes. This Ruddle, though, we *knew* he was our boy, and we still couldn't do anything about it. That was his name, Jacob Ruddle.

"So after the case was marked open, my partner

and I, we couldn't get it out of our heads. Just couldn't get it out of our heads, there wasn't a day one of us didn't bring it up. So eventually we went to this Ruddle and asked him if he'd take a polygraph test. You know what that is?''

"A lie detector?''

"A lie detector. We were completely straight with him, we told him he could refuse to take the test, and we also told him it couldn't be entered in evidence against him, which it can't. I'm not sure that's a good idea, incidentally, but that's the law.

"He agreed to take the test. Don't ask me why. Maybe he thought it would look suspicious of him to refuse, although he must have known we damn well knew he killed her and nothing was going to make him stop looking suspicious to us. Or maybe he honestly thought he could beat the machine. Well, he took the test, and I made sure we had the best operator available to administer the test, and the results were just what we expected.''

"He was guilty?''

"No question about it. It nailed him to the wall, but there was nothing we could do with it. I told him the machine said he was lying. 'Well, those machines must make a few mistakes now and then,' he said, 'because it made one right now.' And he looked me right in the eye, and he knew I didn't believe him, and he knew there was nothing on earth I could do about it.''

"God.''

I went over and sat down next to her again. I sipped some of my drink and closed my eyes for a moment, remembering the look in that bastard's eyes.

"What did you do?''

"My partner and I tossed it back and forth. My partner wanted to put him in the river."

"You mean kill him?"

"Kill him and set him in cement and drop him somewhere in the Hudson."

"You wouldn't do a thing like that."

"I don't know. I might have gone along with it. See, he did it, he killed that girl, and he was an odds-on candidate to do it again sooner or later. Oh, hell, that wasn't all of it. Knowing he did it, knowing he knew we knew he did it, and sending the bastard home. Putting him in the river started sounding like a hell of a good idea, and I might have done it if I hadn't thought of something better."

"What?"

"I had this friend on the narcotics squad. I told him I needed some heroin, a lot of it, and I told him he would be getting every bit of it back. Then one afternoon when Ruddle and his wife were both out of the apartment I let myself in, and I flaked that place as well as it's ever been done. I stuffed smack inside the towel bar, I stuck a can of it in the ball float of his toilet, I put the shit in every really obvious hiding place I could find.

"Then I got back to my friend in narcotics, and I told him I knew where he could make himself a hell of a haul. And he did it right, with a warrant and everything, and Ruddle was upstate in Dannemora before he knew what hit him." I smiled suddenly. "I went to see him between the trial and the sentencing date. His whole defense was that he had no idea how that heroin got there, and not too surprisingly the jury didn't sit up all night worrying about that one. I went to see him and I said,

'You know, Ruddle, it's a shame you couldn't take a lie-detector test. It might make people believe you didn't know where that smack came from.' And he just looked at me because he knew just how it had been done to him and for a change there was nothing *he* could do about it."

"God."

"He drew ten-to-twenty for possession with intent to sell. About three years into his sentence he got in a grudge fight with another inmate and got stabbed to death."

"God."

"The thing is, you wonder just how far you have a right to turn things around like that. Did we have a right to set him up? I couldn't see letting him walk around free, and what other way was there to nail him? But if we couldn't do that, did we have a right to put him in the river? That's a harder one for me to answer. I have a lot of trouble with that one. There must be a line there somewhere, and it's hard to know just where to draw it."

A little while later she said it was getting to be her bedtime.

"I'll go," I said.

"Unless you'd rather stay."

We turned out to be good for each other. For a stitch of time all the hard questions went away and hid in dark places.

Afterward she said that I should stay. "I'll make us breakfast in the morning."

"Okay."

And, sleepily, "Matt? That story you were telling before. About Ruddle?"

"Uh-huh."

"What made you think of it?"

I sort of wanted to tell her, probably for the same reason I'd told her the story in the first place. But part of what I had to do was not tell her, just as I had avoided telling Cale Hanniford.

"Just the similarities in the cases," I said. "Just that it was another case of a girl raped and murdered in the Village, and the one case put me in mind of the other."

She murmured something I couldn't catch. When I was sure she was sleeping soundly, I slipped out of bed and got into my clothes. I walked the couple of blocks to my hotel and went to my room.

I thought I would have trouble sleeping, but it came easier than I expected.

FIFTEEN

The service had just gotten under way when I arrived. I slipped into a rear pew, took a small black book from the rack, and found the place. I'd missed the invocation and the first hymn, but I was in time for the reading of the Law.

He seemed taller than I remembered. Perhaps the pulpit added an impression of height. His voice was rich and commanding, and he spoke the Law with absolute certainty.

"God spake all these words, saying, I am the Lord thy God, which have brought thee out of the land of Egypt, out of the house of bondage.

"Thou shalt have no other gods before Me.

"Thou shalt not make unto thee any graven image, or any likeness of any thing that is in heaven above, or that is in the earth beneath, or that is in the water under the earth; thou shalt not bow down thyself to them, nor serve them, for I the Lord thy God am a jealous God, visiting the iniquity of the fathers upon the third and fourth generation of them that hate Me; and showing

mercy unto thousands of them that love Me, and keep My commandments. . . . "

The room was not crowded. There were perhaps eighty persons present, most of them my age or older, with only a few family groups with children. The church could have accommodated four or five times the number in attendance. I guessed most of the congregation had made the pilgrimage to the suburbs in the past twenty years, their places taken by Irish and Italians whose former neighborhoods were now black and Puerto Rican.

"Honor thy father and thy mother, that thy days may be long upon the land which the Lord thy God giveth thee."

Were there more people in attendance today than normally? Their minister had experienced great personal tragedy. He had not conducted the service the preceding Sunday. This would be their first official glimpse of him since the murder and suicide. Would curiosity bring more of them out? Or would restraint and embarrassment—and the cold air of morning—keep many at home?

"Thou shalt not kill."

Unequivocal statements, these commandments. They brooked no argument. Not *Thou shalt not kill except in special circumstances.*

"Thou shalt not commit adultery. . . . Thou shalt not bear false witness against thy neighbor. . . ."

I rubbed at a pulse point in my temple. Could he see me? I remembered his thick glasses and decided he could not. And I was far in the back, and off to the side.

"Hear also what our Lord Jesus Christ saith: Thou shalt love the Lord thy God with all thy

heart and with all thy soul and with all thy might. This is the first and great commandment. And the second is like unto it. Thou shalt love thy neighbor as thyself. On these two commandments hang all the law and the prophets.''

We stood up and sang a psalm.

The service took a little over an hour. The Old Testament reading was from Isaiah, the New Testament reading from Mark. There was another hymn, a prayer, still another hymn. The offering was taken and consecrated. I put a five on the plate.

The sermon, as promised, dealt with the proposition that the road to Hell was paved with good intentions. It was not enough for us to act with the best and most righteous goals in mind, Martin Vanderpoel told us, because the highest purpose could be betrayed if it were advanced by actions which were not good and righteous in and of themselves.

I didn't pay too much attention to how he elaborated on this because my mind got caught up in the central thesis of the argument and played with it. I wondered whether it was worse for men to do the wrong things for the right reason or the right things for the wrong reason. It wasn't the first time I wondered, or the last.

Then we were standing, and his arms were spread, his robed draping like the wings of an enormous bird, his voice vibrant and resonant.

"The peace of God, which passeth all understanding, keep your hearts and minds in the knowledge and love of God, and of His Son Jesus Christ our Lord; and the blessing of God

Almighty, the Father, and the Son, and the Holy Spirit, be amongst you, and remain with you always. Amen."

Amen.

A few people slipped out of the church without stopping for a few words with Reverend Vanderpoel. The rest lined up for a handshake. I managed to be at the end of the line. When it was finally my turn Vanderpoel blinked at me. He knew my face was familiar, but he couldn't figure out why.

Then he said, "Why, it's Mr. Scudder! I certainly never expected to see you at our services."

"It was enjoyable."

"I'm pleased to hear you say that. I hardly anticipated seeing you again, and I didn't dream of hoping that our incidental meeting might lead you to search for the presence of God." He looked past my shoulder, a half-smile on his lips. "He does work in mysterious ways, does He not?"

"So it seems."

"That a particular tragedy could have this effect upon a person like yourself. I imagine I might find myself using that as a theme for a sermon at some later date."

"I'd like to talk to you, Reverend Vanderpoel. In private, I think."

"Oh, dear," he said. "I'm quite pressed for time today, I'm afraid. I'm sure you have a great many questons about religion, one is always filled with questions that seem to have a great need for immediate answers, but—"

"I don't want to talk about religion, sir."

"Oh?"

"It's about your son and Wendy Hanniford."

"I already told you all that I know."

"I'm afraid I have to tell *you* some things, sir. And we'd better have that conversation now, and it really will have to be private."

"Oh?" He looked at me intently, and I watched the play of emotions on his face. "Very well," he said. "I do have a few tasks that need to be attended to. I'll just be a moment."

I waited, and he wasn't more than ten minutes. Then he took me companionably by the arm and led me through the back of the church and through a door into the rectory. We wound up in the room we had been in before. The electric fire glowed on the hearth, and again he stood in front of it and warmed his long-fingered hands.

"I like a cup of coffee after morning services," he said. "You'll join me?"

"No, thank you."

He left the room and came back with coffee. "Well, Mr. Scudder? What's so urgent?" His tone was deliberately light, but there was tension underneath it.

"I enjoyed the services this morning," I said.

"Yes, so you said, and I'm pleased to hear it. However—"

"I was hoping for a different Old Testament text."

"Isaiah is difficult to grasp, I agree. A poet and a man of vision. There are some interesting commentaries on today's reading if you're interested."

"I was hoping the reading might be from Genesis."

"Oh, we don't start over until Whitsunday, you

know. But why Genesis?"

"A particular portion of Genesis, actually."

"Oh?"

"The Twenty-second Chapter."

He closed his eyes for a moment and frowned in concentration. He opened them and shrugged apologetically. "I used to have a fair memory for chapter and verse. It's been one of the casualties of the aging process, I'm afraid. Shall I look it up?"

I said, " '*And it came to pass after these things, that God did tempt Abraham, and said unto him, Abraham; and he said, Behold, here I am. And he said, Take now thy son, thine only son Isaac, whom thou lovest, and get thee into the land of Moriah; and offer him there for a burnt offering upon one of the mountains which I will tell thee of.*' "

"The temptation of Abraham. '*God will provide himself a lamb for a burnt offering.*' A very beautiful passage." His eyes fixed on me. "It's unusual that you can quote Scripture, Mr. Scudder."

"I had reason to read that passage the other day. It stayed with me."

"Oh?"

"I thought you might care to explain the chapter to me."

"At some other time, certainly, but I scarcely see the urgency of—"

"*Don't you?*"

He looked at me. I got to my feet and took a step toward him. I said, "I think you do. I think you could explain to me the interesting parallels between Abraham and yourself. You could tell me what happens when God doesn't oblige by providing a lamb for the burnt offering. You could tell me more about how the road to Hell is paved with good intentions."

"Mr. Scudder—"

"You could tell me why you were able to murder Wendy Hanniford. And why you let Richie die in your place."

SIXTEEN

"I don't know what you're talking about."

"I think you do, sir."

"My son committed a horrible murder. I'm sure he did not know what he was doing at the moment of his act. I forgive him for what he did, I pray God forgives him—"

"I'm not a congregation, sir. I'm a man who knows all the things you thought no one would ever be able to figure out. Your son never killed anybody until he killed himself."

He sat there for a long moment, taking it all in. He bowed his head a little. His pose was an attitude of prayer, but I don't think he was praying. When he spoke his tone was not defensive so much as it was curious, the words very nearly an admission of guilt.

"What makes you . . . believe this, Mr. Scudder?"

"A lot of things I learned. And the way they all fit together."

"Tell me."

I nodded. I wanted to tell him because I had been feeling the need to tell someone all along. I hadn't told Cale Hanniford. I had come close to telling Trina, had begun hinting at it, but in the end I had not told her, either.

Vanderpoel was the only person I could tell.

I said, "The case was open-and-shut. That's how the police saw it, and it was the only way to see it. But I didn't start out looking for a murderer. I started out trying to learn something about Wendy and your son, and the more I learned, the harder it was for me to buy the idea that he had killed her.

"What nailed him was turning up on the sidewalk covered with blood and behaving hysterically. But if you began to dismiss that from your mind, the whole idea of him being the killer began to break down. He left his job suddenly in the middle of the afternoon. He hadn't planned on leaving. That could have been staged. But instead he came down with a case of indigestion and his employer finally managed to talk him into leaving.

"Then he got home with barely enough time to rape her and kill her and run out into the street. He hadn't been acting oddly during the day. The only thing evidently wrong with him was a stomachache. Theoretically he walked in on her and something about her provoked him into flipping out completely.

"But what was it? A rush of sexual desire? He lived with the girl, and it was a reasonable assumption that he could make love to her any time he wanted to. And the more I learned about him, the more certain I became that he never made love to her. They lived together, but they didn't sleep together."

"What makes you say that?"

"Your son was homosexual."

"That is not true."

"I'm afraid it is."

"Relations between men are an abomination in the eyes of God."

"That may be. I'm no authority. Richie was homosexual. He wasn't comfortable with it. I gather it was impossible for him to be comfortable with any kind of sexuality. He had very mixed-up feelings about you, about his mother, and they. made any real sexual relationship impossible."

I walked over to the fake fire. I wondered if the fireplace was fake, too. I turned and looked at Martin Vanderpoel. He had not changed position. He was still sitting in his chair with his hands on his knees, his eyes on the patch of rug between his feet.

I said, "Richie seems to have been stabilized by his relationship with Wendy Hanniford. He was able to regulate his life, and I'd guess he was relatively happy. Then he came home one afternoon, and something set him reeling. Now what would do that?"

He didn't say anything.

"He might have walked in and found her with another man. But that didn't add up because why would it upset him that much? He must have known how she supported herself, that she saw other men during the afternoons while he was at work. Besides, there would have to be some trace of that other man. He wouldn't just run off when Richie started slicing with a razor.

"And where would Richie get a razor? He used an electric. Nobody twenty years old shaves with a straight razor anymore. Some kids carry razors the way other kids carry knives, but Richie wasn't that kind of kid.

"And what did he do with the razor afterward? The cops decided he flipped it out the window or dropped it somewhere and somebody picked it up and walked off with it."

"Isn't that plausible, Mr. Scudder?"

"Uh-huh. If he had a razor in the first place. And it was also possible he'd used a knife instead of a razor. There were plenty of knives in the kitchen. But I was in that kitchen, and all the cupboards and drawers were neatly closed, and you don't grab up a knife to slaughter someone in a fit of passion and remember to close the drawer carefully behind you. No, there was only one way it made sense to me. Richie came home and found Wendy already dead or dying, and that knocked him for a loop. He couldn't handle it."

My headache was coming back again. I rubbed at my temple with a knuckle. It didn't do much good.

"You told me Richie's mother died when he was quite young."

"Yes."

"You didn't tell me she killed herself."

"How did you learn that?"

"When something's a matter of record, sir, anyone can find out about it if he takes the trouble to look for it. I didn't have to dig for that information. All I had to do was think of looking for it. Your wife killed herself in the bathtub by slashing her wrists. Did she use a razor?"

He looked at me.

"Your razor, sir?"

"I don't see that it matters."

"Don't you?" I shrugged. "Richie walked in and found his mother dead in a pool of blood. Then, fourteen years later, he walked into an apartment on Bethune Street and found the woman he was living with dead in her bed. Also slashed with a razor, and also lying in a pool of blood.

"I suppose Wendy Hanniford was a mother to him in certain ways. They must have played a lot of different surrogate roles in each other's lives. But all of a sudden Wendy became his dead mother, and Richie couldn't handle it, and he wound up doing something I guess he'd never been able to do before."

"What?"

"He had intercourse with her. It was a pure, uncontrollable reaction. He didn't even take time to take his clothes off. He fell on her and he had intercourse with her, and when it was over he ran out into the streets and started screaming his lungs out because his head was full of the fact that he had had intercourse with his mother and now she was dead. You can see what he thought, sir. He thought he fucked her to death."

"God," he said.

I wondered if he'd ever pronounced it quite that way before.

My headache was getting worse. I asked him if I could have some aspirins. He told me how to find the first-floor lavatory. There were aspirin tablets in the medicine cabinet. I took two and drank half a glass of water.

When I went back into the living room he hadn't changed position. I sat down in my chair and looked at him. There was a lot more and we would get to it, but I wanted to wait for him to pick it up.

He said, "This is extraordinary, Mr. Scudder."

"Yes."

"I never even considered the possibility that Richard was innocent. I just assumed he had done it. If what you think is true—"

"It's true."

"Then he died for nothing."

"He died for you, sir. He was the lamb for the burnt offering."

"You can't seriously believe I killed that girl."

"I know you did, sir."

"How can you possibly know that?"

"You met Wendy in the spring."

"Yes. I believe I told you that the last time you were here."

"You picked a time when you knew Richie would be at work. You wanted to meet this girl because you were bothered at the idea of Richie living in sin with her."

"I already told you as much."

"Yes, you did." I took a breath. "Wendy Hanniford was very strongly drawn to older men, men who functioned as father figures for her. She was aggressive in situations involving a man who attracted her. She managed to seduce several of her professors at college.

"She met you, and she was attracted to you. It's not hard to imagine why. You're a very commanding figure of a man. Very stern and forbidding. And on top of everything you were Richie's actual father, and she and Richie were living like brother and sister.

"So she made a play for you. I gather she was very good at getting her point across. And you were very vulnerable. You'd been a widower for a good many years. Your housekeeper may have been very efficient at her appointed tasks, but you certainly couldn't have picked her as a potential sexual outlet. The last time you were here you told me you felt in retrospect that you should have remarried for Richie's sake. I think you were really saying that you should have remarried for your own sake, so that you wouldn't have been vulnerable to Wendy Hanniford."

"This is all guesswork on your part, Mr. Scudder."

"You went to bed with her. Maybe that was the first time you went to bed with anybody since your wife died. I wouldn't know, and it doesn't much matter. But you went to bed with her and I guess you liked it because you kept going back. You thought it was a sin, but that didn't change things much because you went right on sinning.

"You certainly hated her. Even after she was dead you made it a point to tell me how evil she was. I thought at the time you were justifying your son's act. I didn't believe then that he did it, but I believed *you* thought so.

"Then you told me he admitted his guilt."

He didn't say anything. I watched him wipe perspiration from his forehead, then wipe his hand on his robe.

"That didn't have to mean anything. You might have been talking yourself into the belief that Richie died penitent. Or he could well have admitted it to you because he could have become sufficiently confused after the fact. Everything was

175

jumbled up for him. He told his lawyer he found Wendy dead in the bathtub. A little more reflection and he must have decided that he had killed her even if he couldn't remember it.

"But the more I found out about Wendy, the harder it was to picture her as evil. I don't doubt she had an evil effect on the lives of certain other people. But why would she *seem* evil to you? There was really only one explanation for that, sir. She made you want to do something you were ashamed of. And that made you do something more shameful. You killed her.

"You planned it. You took your razor along. And you had sex with her one final time before you murdered her."

"That's a lie."

"It's not. I can even tell you what you did. The autopsy showed that she had had both oral and vaginal intercourse shortly before death. Richie would have had genital intercourse with her, so what you did, sir, was take off all your clothes and let her perform fellatio upon you, and then you whipped out your razor and slashed her to death, and then you went home and let your son hang himself for it."

I stood up and planted my feet in front of his chair. "I'll tell you what I think. I think you're a son of a bitch. You knew Richie would be home from work in another couple of hours. You knew he'd discover the body. You didn't necessarily know he'd go nuts, but you knew the cops would grab him and lean on him hard. You set him up for it."

"No!"

"No?"

"I was going to . . . to call the police. I was going to report the crime anonymously. They would have found the body while he was still at work. They would have known he had nothing to do with it, they would have blamed it on some anonymous sex partner of hers. They never would have thought—"

"Why didn't you follow through?"

He fought to catch his breath. He said, "I left the apartment. My head was reeling, I was . . . badly shaken by what I had done. And then I saw Richie on his way home. He didn't see me. I saw him mount the stairs, and I knew . . . I knew it was too late. He was already on the scene."

"So you let him go upstairs."

"Yes."

"And when you went to see him in jail?"

"I wanted to tell him. I wanted to . . . to say something to him. I . . . I couldn't."

He leaned forward and put his head in his hands.

I let him sit like that for a while. He didn't sob, didn't make a sound, just sat there looking somewhere into the black parts of his soul. Finally I got up and took a half-pint flask of bourbon from my pocket. I uncapped it and offered it to him.

He wasn't having any. "I don't use spirits, Mr. Scudder."

"Think of it as a special occasion."

"I don't use spirits. I don't allow them in my house."

I thought about that and decided he wasn't in a position to set rules. I took a long drink.

He said, "You can't prove any of this."

"Are you sure of that?"

"Some conjecture on your part. A great deal of it, as a matter of fact."

"So far you haven't refuted any of it."

"No, if anything I've confirmed it, haven't I? But I'll deny having said any such thing to you. You haven't the slightest bit of truth."

"You're absolutely right."

"Then I don't see what you're driving at."

"I can't prove anything. The cops will be able to, though, when I go to them. They never had any reason to dig before. But they'll start digging, and they'll turn something up. They'll start by asking you to account for your movements on the day of the murder. You won't be able to. That's nothing in and of itself, but it's enough to encourage them to keep looking. They've still got that apartment sealed off. They never had a reason to dust it for prints. They'll have a reason now, and they'll find your prints somewhere. I'm sure you didn't run around wiping surfaces.

"They'll ask to see your razor. If you bought a new one since then, they'll wonder why. They'll go through all your wardrobe, looking for blood-stains. I guess you had your clothes off when you killed her, but you'll have gotten traces of blood on something or other and it won't all wash out.

"They'll put a case together a piece at a time, and they won't even need a full case because you'll crack under questioning in no time at all. You'll crack wide open."

"I may be stronger than you seem to think, Mr. Scudder."

"You're not strong so much as you're rigid. You'll break. I couldn't tell you how many suspects I've questioned. It gives you a pretty good idea of who's going to crack easy. You'd be a cinch.''

He looked at me, then averted his eyes.

''But it doesn't matter whether you crack or not, and it doesn't matter whether they put a solid case together or not, because all they have to do is start looking and you've had it. Take a look at your life, Reverend Vanderpoel. Once they start, you're finished. You won't be up there on the pulpit Sunday mornings reading the Law to your congregation. You'll be disgraced.''

He sat for a few minutes in silence. I took out my flask and had another drink. Drinking was against his religion. Well, murder was against mine.

''What do you want, Mr. Scudder? I have to tell you that I'm not a rich man.''

''Pardon me?''

''I suppose I could arrange regular payments. I couldn't afford very much, but I could—''

''I don't want money.''

''You're not trying to blackmail me?''

''No.''

He frowned at me, puzzled. ''Then I don't understand.''

I let him think about it.

''You haven't gone to the police?''

''No.''

''Do you intend to go to them?''

''I hope I won't have to.''

''I don't understand what you mean.''

I took another little drink. I capped the flask and put it back in my pocket. From another pocket I took a small vial of pills.

I said, "I found these in the medicine cabinet at the Bethune Street apartment. They were Richie's. He had them prescribed fifteen months ago. They're Seconal, sleeping pills.

"I don't know if Richie had trouble sleeping or not, but he evidently didn't take any of these. The bottle's still full. There are thirty pills. I think he bought them with the intention of committing suicide. A lot of people make false starts like that. Sometimes they throw the pills away when they change their minds. Other times they keep them around in order to simplify things if they decide to kill themselves at a later date. And there are people who find some security in having the means of suicide close at hand. They say thoughts of self-destruction get people through a great many bad nights."

I walked over to him and placed the vial on the little table beside his chair.

"There are enough there," I said. "If a person were to take them all and go to bed, he wouldn't wake up."

He looked at me. "You have everything all worked out."

"Yes. I haven't been able to think of much else."

"You expect me to end my life."

"Your life is over, sir. It's just a question of how it finishes up."

"And if I take these pills?"

"You leave a note. You're despondent over the death of your son, and you can't find it within yourself to go on living. It won't be that far from the truth, will it?"

"And if I refuse?"

"I go to the police Tuesday morning."

He breathed deeply several times. Then he said, "Do you honestly think it would be so bad to let me go on living my life, Mr. Scudder? I perform a valuable function, you know. I'm a good minister."

"Perhaps you are."

"I honestly think I do some good in this world. Not a great deal, but some. Is it illogical for me to want to go on doing good?"

"No."

"And I am not a criminal, you know. I did kill . . . that girl."

"Wendy Hanniford."

"I killed her. Oh, you're so quick to see it as a calculated, cold-blooded act, aren't you? Do you know how many times I swore not to see her again? Do you know how many nights I lay awake, wrestling with demons? Do you even know how many times I went to her apartment with my razor in my pocket, torn between the desire to slay her and the fear of committing such a monstrous sin? Do you know any of that?"

I didn't say anything.

"I killed her. Whatever happens, I will never kill anyone again. Can you honestly say I constitute a danger to society?"

"Yes."

"How?"

"It's bad for society when murders remain unpunished."

"But if I do as you suggest, no one will know I've taken my life for that reason. No one will know I was punished for murder."

"I'll know."

"You'd be judge and jury, then. Is that right?"

"No. You will, sir."

He closed his eyes, leaned back in his chair. I wanted another drink, but I let the flask stay in my pocket. The headache was still there. The aspirin hadn't even touched it.

"I regard suicide as a sin, Mr. Scudder."

"So do I."

"You do?"

"Absolutely. If I didn't I probably would have killed myself years ago. There are worse sins."

"Murder."

"That's one of them."

He fixed his eyes on me. "Do you think I am an evil man, Mr. Scudder?"

"I'm not an expert on that. Good and evil. I have a lot of trouble figuring those things out."

"Answer my question."

"I think you've had good intentions. You were talking about that earlier."

"And I've paved a road to Hell?"

"Well, I don't know where the road leads, but there are a lot of wrecks along the highway, aren't there? Your wife committed suicide. Your mistress got slashed to death. Your son went crazy and hanged himself for something he didn't do. Does that make you good or evil? You'll have to work that one out for yourself."

"You intend to go to the police Tuesday morning."

"If I have to."

"And otherwise you'll keep your silence."

"Yes."

"Ah, and what about you, Mr. Scudder? Are you a force for good or evil? I'm sure you've asked yourself the question."

"Now and then."

"How do you answer it?"

"Ambivalently."

"And now, in this act? Forcing me to kill myself?"

"That's not what I'm doing."

"Isn't it?"

"No. I'm allowing you to kill yourself. I think you're a damned fool if you don't, but I'm not forcing you to do anything."

SEVENTEEN

I was awake early Monday morning. I got a *Times* at the corner and read it over bacon and eggs and coffee. A cabdriver had been murdered in East Harlem. Someone had stuck an icepick into him through one of the air holes in his partition. Now everyone who read the *Times* would know a new way to score off a cabdriver.

I walked over to the bank when it opened and deposited half of Cale Hanniford's thousand-dollar check. I took the rest in cash, then walked a few blocks to the post office and bought a money order for a few hundred dollars. I addressed an envelope in my hotel room, put a stamp on it, picked up the phone and called Anita.

I said, "I'm sending you a couple of bucks."

"You don't have to do that."

"Well, to pick out something for the boys. How have they been?"

"Fine, Matt. They're in school now, of course. They'll be sorry they missed your call."

"It's never much good over the phone, anyway.

I was thinking, I could get tickets for the Mets game Friday night. If you could get them to the Coliseum I could send them home in a cab. If you think they'd like to go."

"I know they would. I could drive them there with no trouble."

"Well, I'll see if I can pick up tickets. They shouldn't be too hard to come by."

"Should I tell them, or should I wait until you actually have the tickets? Or do you want to tell them yourself?"

"No, you tell them. In case they have something else lined up.

"They'd cancel anything to see the game with you."

"Well, not if it's something important."

"They could even go back to the city with you. You could rent them a room at your hotel and put them on the train the next day."

"We'll see."

"All right. How have you been, Matt?"

"Fine. You?"

"All right."

"Things about the same with you and George?"

"Why?"

"Just wondered."

"We're still seeing each other if that's what you mean."

"He thinking about getting a divorce from Rosalie?"

"We don't talk about it. Matt, I've got to go, they're honking for me."

"Sure."

"And let me know about the tickets."

"Sure."

It wasn't in the early *Post*, but around two in the afternoon I had the radio on to one of the all-news stations and they had it. The Reverend Martin Vanderpoel, minister of the First Reformed Church of Bay Ridge, had been found dead in his bedroom by his housekeeper. The death had been tentatively attributed, pending autopsy, to the voluntary ingestion of an overdose of barbiturates. Reverend Vanderpoel was identified as the father of Richard Vanderpoel, who had recently hanged himself after having been arrested for the murder of Wendy Hanniford in the apartment the two had shared in Greenwich Village. Reverend Vanderpoel was reported to have been profoundly despondent over his son's death, and this despondency had evidently led him to take his own life.

I turned off the radio and sat around for half an hour or so. Then I walked around the block to St. Paul's and put a hundred dollars in the poor box, a tenth of what I'd received as a bonus from Cale Hanniford.

I sat near the back for a while, thinking about a lot of things.

Before I left I lit four candles. One for Wendy, one for Richie, the usual one for Estrellita Rivera.

And one for Martin Vanderpoel, of course.